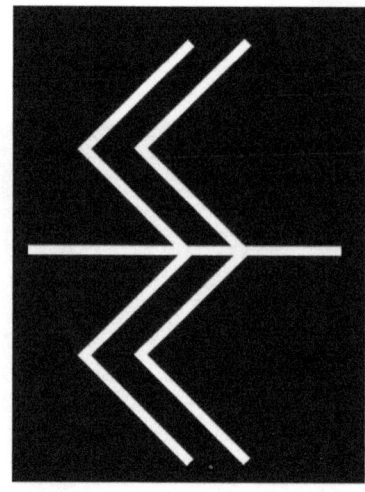

A Broken River Books Original
Broken River Books
Oklahoma City, OK

ISBN: 978-1-940885-56-8

Printed in the USA.

BLACK GYPSIES

(slowed & throwed edition)

by
Grant Wamack

BROKEN RIVER BOOKS
OKLAHOMA CITY, OK

Dedicated to Isaac Kirkman.
Hope I made you proud, man.

"The winter will ask what we did all summer."
-Gypsy Proverb

1.
Tatted Like a Biker Boy

The day Marcus got his first piece of ink, someone shot the shop to shit.

Warped synths, tittering hi-hats, and an ocean of bass flooded the cramped tattoo shop. Faded posters of inked rappers, black celebs, and athletes hugged the walls like a second membrane. Five clients sprawled out in leather chairs, irons buzzing like a hornet's nest.

A steady, gloved hand sloped downward in an elegant arc, carving the word "JACKBOY" in jagged letters with beautiful black Japanese anemones blooming in the background of the brown canvas draped across the chair's arm.

Reginald "Jazz" Harris adjusted his grip on the gun, and a dull pain rose up his forearm. He rotated his wrist in small circles, trying to work the pain out.

"Damn carpal tunnel acting up again," he muttered under his breath.

Marcus sat in his chair, phone in hand, observing the fresh ink penetrating his epidermis, five layers deep in melanin-rich flesh. "What's that?" he asked.

"Nothing you need to be concerned about, young man."

Reginald was a lean black man with a receding hairline (lined up to perfection), inviting dimples, and a goatee. He'd worked at this shop for twenty years, a walking history book, twenty years of being exposed to the steady influx of gentrification, gerrymandering, crime, and political stratagems that had reshaped the landscape around him. The shades of brown in the neighborhood had become lighter and lighter throughout the years, but that didn't stop the clientele from being primarily black, coming from all over Chicago to get inked by the notorious artists housed in this space.

Looking up at the flat-screen TV, Reginald's eyes became hyper-focused. His left arm tensed, his brow furrowed.

"Fuck, turn that shit down," he yelled out. He knew this was a prelude to an oncoming headache.

Someone yelled back incoherently and Lucki's "4 The Betta" softened and the cries of football commentators bounced off the walls, but not before Reginald had to put in his two cents.

"Fuckin Packers. Bunch of fu-fu niggas think they know how to run the ball."

The score read 12-6. The Bears were up and the Packers were moving to the 15-yard line. Reginald squeezed Marcus' shoulder, watching the TV intently. A sea of yellow and green swam across the screen. A running back juked past the Bears' safety and backpedaled into the endzone. The crowd erupted into a frenzy of cheers and boos.

Reginald's eyes widened and he pricked the young man in front of him. Too much pressure on the needle. He saw the pain register in the kid's face, but he didn't say anything about it. The kid had some ice in his veins.

"Did you see that shit? Refs didn't even call the flag. Must be sliding them some paper on the side."

Marcus' brown eyes were glued to the screen. "It's crazy. We were just up by six in the second quarter. They really need to do something about Cutler. He's bringing our team down and everyone with him."

"You can't put all the blame on Cutler. Football's a team sport. Just a little too much funk in his hands and a loose ego."

Someone turned the music back up. Post Malone's "Too Young." The DJ on Shade 45 brought the song to a skidding halt 30 seconds in, added some scratches, and reversed the track back to the beginning.

Counting bands, hallejuah.

Marcus nodded along to the song.

"You actually like this?" Reginald asked.

"It's fire."

"It's cool, but it doesn't have any soul in it. Misses that certain something that makes a song kick you inside your core. It's almost *there*… but tries way too hard."

"I get it," Marcus sighed. "I need some jazz in my life."

"Exactly. I'm going to give you a CD next time I see you."

Marcus rolled his eyes. "You could just give me a list of

names and songs, and I'll be able to stream them. This isn't 1992. We have D-S-P's."

"I don't give two shits about D-S-P's, Jackboy. And you better watch your mouth. I could fuck up your entire tattoo with one swoop."

"Okay, okay. On foenem, I'll listen to some jazz one of these days. I'm just saying you don't have to waste all that energy bringing a CD. It could save you some time. Plus, I don't even own a CD player."

Reginald grunted, coming back down to reality, remembering that most cars were far beyond his outdated technology.

"Luke, you alright over there?"

Lucas Reynolds removed the sports magazine from his face and grimaced. "No, I'm fuckin heated. I put down $500 on this game. Really thought I'd be able to invest my money back into crypto."

"Bitcoin's the way to go," Marcus said.

"I personally like the good ole fashioned American dollar," Reginald said. "Something tangible, something I can feel and touch. Something that can't get hacked."

"I have some Ethereum and Litecoin that's doing decent," said Lucas. "But man, Bitcoin's going to be outta here in a few years. I'll move to Canada or Switzerland. Somewhere quiet and somewhere I can be sovereign and free."

"I feel you," said Marcus.

"Here you go with that Hotep shit," Reginald said. "Chicago is home. I don't know why people are always moving.

There's so much history here."

Lucas tossed the magazine down on the table. "Look at the news. It's a shithole. The education system is trash, the crime-rate's crazy and the kids are killing everything in sight just cuz it's hot outside. The mayor doesn't give a shit and they're threatening to call in the National Guard." He fished a pack of cigarettes out of his front pocket and exited the shop.

Reginald shook his head. "He needs a hobby outside of doing tattoos all day. The ink can go to your head. Make you start thinking funny."

Reginald returned his focus to filling in the Y, making sure his strokes were sharp and steady. He could feel the skin ripping underneath his needle's tip. Knew it had to hurt like a bitch. Wondered how much pain Marcus could stomach.

"You got any tissues?" Marcus asked.

Reginald paused and handed a box over to Marcus so he could grab a few.

The music transitioned and Marcus began nodding to the addictive rhythm. Lil Durk's auto-tuned voice spread through the shop.

Fuck your life, I won't think twice.

"This shit bangs," Marcus said before blowing his nose.

Pop. Pop. Pop.

Gunshots rata-tatted through the summer afternoon. A bullet ricocheted off the counter. Glass shattered, shards flying through the air like Japanese cherry blossoms. Tires screeched and yells became distorted words floating in the atmosphere.

Reginald tossed his tattoo gun aside and covered his head with his hands and muttered a soft prayer as he sank down to the floor.

Marcus ducked down next to Reginald, his right leg shaking.

Time slowed to a jelly-like consistency, catching everyone in its wake. Wide eyes glanced toward the windows, willing the bullets to stay away from the shop, waiting, waiting, waiting....

Music still spilled out the speakers, and the commentator spoke on the TV.

"It's a sad day for Bears fans and a much sadder day for Chicagoans."

Traffic rushed past, blurs of mustard yellow and blue zooming by. Someone yelled from across the street. A woman started crying hysterically. Reginald slowly stood up, patting his chest down for bullet holes and phantom blood. Heart beating like a jackhammer in his chest, he struggled to find the vape pen in his pocket. Hands shaking, he fished the device out, dropping it on the ground.

"You okay Marcus?"

Marcus stood up like a zombie on unsteady legs. He looked like he had seen the boogeyman. Bags under his eyes. His thumb digging into the center of his palm. He leaned against the wall and vomited. Stumbling over to the sink, he rinsed out his mouth. Gagging, he spit out the rest of his breakfast into the drain.

"I'll clean that up," Marcus said, catching his breath.

Reginald waved him aside. "No need. I got it. You alright though?"

"Alright enough."

"Okay, good. Just have a seat and relax while I clean up."

6

"Maybe that's a good idea..."

Reginald took a sharp inhale and coughed. He inspected the pen in his fingers, wondering how much closer this was bringing him to death. His doctor said it was a lot better than cigarettes and that his lungs would thank him for it later.

Healthy. Only reason he did it. To prolong his health and hopefully extend his years with his daughter.

The vape slipped out of his fingers and fell to the ground again.

"Need to take my own advice and sit my old ass down."

Reginald brushed the dirt off the hem of his Bears jersey. It was his favorite. Devin Hester had complimented him on it last year when Reginald had attended a game against the Patriots. Blew 'em out the water.

Reginald usually grinned whenever he thought back to that warm day, but this was different. Now he was on the verge of tears. He grabbed a towel and ran it under cold water and wiped his face.

Reginald felt drained. Exhausted. Empty and hollow. He had to go visit his brother's grave soon. Pay respect. Maybe sit down and have a cigarette with him like old times. Tell him about the game. He'd like that.

Tattoos gave Reginald an outlet for his anger and the hopelessness creeping into his heart. Used to be music that would stir something in him creatively, serving as the catalyst for inspiration, but that went down the drain once his mom couldn't afford to continue paying for his lessons. His fingers still remembered the pedals on the saxophone.

He missed playing. Always told himself he'd get back into it, but the years kept passing by. Tattooing remained a passion though. Something that got him through the hard times. Almost felt like his purpose.

Almost.

Reginald stretched his shoulders. Upper back muscles cracking. Time to get back to work, he told himself. Work's good. Keeps your head clear.

"Marcus…maybe you should head home. I'm sure your momma's worried sick about you."

"No, you're almost done. I rather you finish."

"Alright."

He added the final details to Marcus' arm, squinting at the artistic font.

He knew the boy was shook. He could see it in his eyes, the way they looked at the tattoo for a second and darted back to the window. Replaying the moment over and over on a continuous loop.

"You alright?"

"Yeah. Just processing."

With steady hands, Reginald gripped the tattoo gun and went back to work. He could've said it was finished a half hour ago, but he took a certain pleasure in his craft and his details are what really popped and brought in new clients. Reminded him of jazz. It didn't have to be technically perfect or sound. Just had to hit the right notes on the canvas.

"There we go," he said twenty minutes later. He wrapped Marcus' arm in Saran wrap. Then he gave him a handful of moisturizer packets and a hearty pat on the back. "Make sure you get some good sleep, and no working out. Don't want an infection."

Police sirens rang in the distance like ominous church bells.

Marcus stood in front of the mirror and inspected his tattoo. "That's legit."

"Ayeeeee. Now where's my money at, nigga?" Reginald furrowed his brow and tossed his plastic gloves into the trash bin. He cleared his throat.

Marcus pulled out three balled up hundred-dollar bills.

"Keep the change."

Reginald straightened the bills and held them up to the sunlight, squinting to make sure they weren't counterfeit. A couple of fellas came through a few weeks ago and tried to pull a fast one on him. He had to bust their heads in. Ever since that day, he kept his steel baseball bat within arm's reach and a .44 magnum pistol in the back just in case things ever spun out of control.

"Make sure you stay out of trouble. We don't need to lose anyone else around here. You're family."

"I got you, Reg." Marcus pulled on his t-shirt, covering his broad chest, and headed toward the door. "I'll be safe. Promise."

"I'm serious, now. Don't let that ink go to your head. I know what you get into." He looked into Marcus' eyes and wondered how many more years he had left. Shaking his head, he hoped the youngin would make it past 21--the first of many ethereal checkpoints for surviving in Chicago.

"On foenem, I got you," Marcus yelled as he exited. The

brass bell attached to the door jingled.

"Hard-headed nigga," Reginald said. He shook his head and grabbed a mop to clean up the vomit drying on the floor.

Someone shouldered past Marcus, crying.

"Luke got shot."

2.
A Crossroad of Sorts

Marcus hurried up the steps visibly shaken, taking two at a time, but still excited about the new art covering his forearm. He felt official. Couldn't wait to tell Gordo later. Sliding his key into the lock, he heard a distinctive *click* and opened the door.

Mom lounged in the living room with her soaps up extra loud. An oblong shadow in a worn recliner, soft glow of the television glinting off her glasses. She called her son into the living room.

"Come in here. Let me get a good look at you."

Marcus wished like hell he'd have worn a hoodie to cover the fresh ink on his arms. He felt exposed and vulnerable to the storm slowly swelling in the living room.

His mom wore a loose-fitting gown, her black hair tied back into a high-top ponytail. Eyes fixated on the TV.

Arm out like a stop sign. "Wait a minute now," she said. "It's just now getting good."

Marcus stood there, awkwardly watching a Latin man seduce

11

a brunette. He held his arms behind his back, hands fidgeting.

"Oh chile, it's getting hot in here." His mom fanned herself with a stack of bills.

"Mom."

The man on the screen pulled the brunette in close, hands wrapped around her thin waist and kissed her deeply. Then the soap opera transitioned into commercials.

"What's that garbage on your arm?"

"It's a tattoo."

"Don't get smart with me. Come here," she gestured with the stack of mail.

Marcus groaned. He needed to save more money and stop wasting it on shoes. He had to get out of here and move into his own crib. This shit was too much.

His mom yanked his wrist, nearly pulling it out the socket.

"Jackboy. What the hell does that mean? Is that gang terminology or something? What I tell you about these gangs? They're nothing but-"

"Hol up, hol up. It's not a gang," he held his hands out like white flags. "Just something me and Gordo decided to get. Represents our bond, our connection."

"'Bond,'" his mom spit the word out like phlegm. "That boy is no good. Got too much Panamanian in his blood. That's why he's always walking around here looking confused."

"Mom. He's black."

"I don't care what he is. You don't need to be hanging around him. He might as well have a gang inside that fat stomach of his."

Marcus sighed. "It's more than a tattoo. It's art."

"Art? Art is something you hang up on wall or a museum. You got some nerve strolling in here with that trash on *my arm.*"

"Your arm? Last time I checked, this is my body."

"What did I tell you about that slick mouth of yours, boy? I'll still smack the black off you. Don't test me, chile."

"I'm sorry, ma'am."

"You look sorry. Now get out my face. I might have to pray on this. Lord have mercy."

Marcus went to his room, feeling the tension building in his jaw and the stress climbing up his spine. He clenched his hands and took a deep breath and exhaled. He closed the door behind him and kicked off his shoes. He stuck his phone on the charger and laid down.

Gotta clean those smudges off, he thought, staring at his shoes at the foot of his bed.

He eased into the warmth of the bed, not realizing how sleepy he felt. The gunshots rang through his memory, forever imprinted into his psyche. Glass shattering on repeat. He shook his head and his eyelids grew heavy. He allowed the darkness to take him under.

His phone vibrated, slightly muffled by the carpet. He ignored it, easing deeper into the soft darkness. The unanswered texts nibbled at his thoughts and he rolled over with a groan.

He picked up his phone and blinked away the blurriness and stared at the cracked screen. It was a text from Gordo. "We got work, bro bro."

Marcus grinned and texted him back. "Be outside in 5."

Marcus fell asleep on the L, oblivious to train's fast trek. The entire world jerked into focus the moment he snapped his eyes open. He wiped the drool hanging from his mouth. A watercolor blur of towering skyscrapers, magnolia trees, and expensive high rises swam by like a vibrant shape-shifting beast. He sniffled and cracked his neck. Shaking off the cobwebs from half-remembered dreams, he was struck by a paranoid sense of dislocation.

He checked his pockets, making sure no one helped themselves to what was inside. He refused to be caught lacking.

A trio of hipster high school girls laughed and snickered. They had their smart phones in hand, snapping photos and recording snippets of video.

Marcus realized his ass was most certainly being uploaded to the internet and being served as today's quick ten seconds of entertainment.

He snapped. "Fuck are you taking pictures for?"

One girl's blue eyes grew wide behind her blocky glasses. She looked to her friends for back up. They played dumb, looking away while putting their phones back into their purses and bags. A peroxide blonde with curls-most likely the ringleader-shoved a thick piece of gum into her mouth.

"We're not doing anything wrong. It's public domain."

"Bitch, do I look like I'm in a *public domain* type of mood?"

Her thin lips tightened into a glossy crease, and she looked down at her phone. Fingers typing rapidly.

Marcus looked around the train at the other passengers. Most of them seemed unconcerned, but a couple of older folks eyed him. He stared right back and glared. They looked away, acting as if nothing had happened.

That's right, he thought. *Mind your business.*

Checking his phone, he realized he missed his stop and he'd have to get off at the next one if he wanted to make it home and not get cussed out.

The train shuddered to a stop. A loud beep made his ears ring. The steel doors slid open with a cool *hiss.* He walked by the girls and they curled their legs inward, making room for his passage.

The wind ruffled Marcus' hair. He threw his oversized hood over his head, protecting his immaculate waves. He made his way through West Garfield Park, hands shoved in his pockets. He passed by a number of boarded up businesses, empty lots, and brick homes that seemed to have been deserted for as long as he could remember.

A group of black men ranging from mid-teens to early-twenties hung outside a weathered yellow brick apartment building. Bass-heavy drill music spilled out an open window on the first floor. A few of them blocked the sidewalk ahead.

A blue light affixed to a pole was flashing across the street. He hated those lights because of the cops, but in this moment, it was a beacon of danger. A clear signal that he'd fucked up and ended up in the wrong neighborhood.

Feeling several glassy eyes watching his approach, Marcus wrapped his hand around the switchblade in his pocket. He massaged the cold hilt between his sweaty thumb and index finger. He'd stolen it from his Uncle Jimmy a couple months after he nearly lost his life to some Vice Lords.

A tall-ass nigga, dressed in all black, emerged from the center of the group. He mean-mugged Marcus through red-eyed slits nearly covered by long dreads and a cloud of smoke. A six-pointed star with two pitchforks was tatted above his right eyebrow and a heart with wings kissed his neck.

A chill ran up the base of Marcus' neck. He blamed it on the wind. Knowing good and well the man standing in front of him was the source of his unease.

"Aye nigga, come smoke with us," the dreadhead said, inviting him closer to his circle of smoke floating around his head.

Marcus hesitated. He thought about shoving through the makeshift huddle, but knew that was the wrong move. His gut continued to yell at him—*keep on moving*—but his gut failed to see how tricky the situation at hand was.

It had been a long day and a couple puffs wouldn't hurt. Plus, he'd run out of weed a couple nights ago and his plug wasn't hitting him back.

"What you smoking on?" Marcus asked.

The dreadhead took a sharp pull on the blunt, tilted his head backward and blew smoke at a sharp angle.

"That loud, nigga. What else?" The dreadhead grinned, revealing a set of white teeth that seemed too big for his mouth.

Marcus shrugged and took the blunt. He inspected it before taking a hit, and coughed into his fist.

A chubby nigga and a man with a black beanie laughed, tears in their eyes.

"Damn, you weren't ready," the dreadhead said, taking the blunt back. "Told you this loud wasn't no joke. Don't know why people think I'm lying. I'm a man of my word."

"Naw, this is some good shit." Marcus coughed again. "Just wasn't ready."

The nigga wearing the beanie chimed in. "I could see that."

"Whatchu you getting into tonight?" the dreadhead asked, passing the blunt to his right. "You got a thot waiting?"

Marcus wished that was the case. "Naw, nothing special. Just going home and coolin."

"Where's that?" The dreadhead's eyes glowed even though the sun was beginning to set on the horizon.

Marcus knew the dreadhead was a Gangster Disciple based off the ink on his face, the black hoodie and jeans, and his off-kilter stance. A GD through and through.

"Eastside." It was a bold-faced lie, but people called Marcus "Ice" for a reason. He never faltered under pressure or heat no matter how persistent the application.

"Hmph," the dreadhead said, looking Marcus up and down. "Is that so? I got some cousins out that way. Family. You know Jo Jo or Rasheed?"

"Naw, can't say I have."

"Alright, well I've never seen you in these parts. Just wondering how you got so far from home? Still, you look real familiar. You're not a Black Stone or Hustla are you? Because if there's one thing I hate more than anything in this world, it's those Stone niggas."

"Naw, I'm not a Stone or Hustla. Not my type of people."

"Not your type of people?" The dreadhead tasted the words, chewing on them. "Well I don't take kindly to liars. Not saying you're a liar or anything. I'm just sayin..."

"What I got to lie about?"

"Good question."

The chubby nigga chuckled and the dreadhead turned around so fast, the instigator threw his hands in the air, preparing for a blow that never came.

"Excuse my nigga over here. He's a bit messy, and fat as hell. Eats the gossip, literally."

Marcus shot a glance at the time on his phone. It was starting to get late. He didn't want to get caught up.

"Before we were interrupted, I just wanted to know if a fine upstanding gentleman like ya self would lie to me? We shared a blunt together. That's sacred, my nigga."

Marcus shifted his weight. "Nigga, I'm not lying. How many times I gotta tell you?"

"You getting real defensive, my nigga. I was just asking a few questions...but maybe you're right. Everyone deserves the benefit of the doubt. You said Hustlas and Stones aren't you're type of people. Who are your type of people?"

"Folks."

The dreadhead nodded, shaking his head up and down. "Okay. So you're a Folk. That's good and all, but that kinda adds some complications to the situation at hand."

Marcus eased into his high, but anxiety balled up in his stomach.

What's this nigga's aim?

"You look confused. Let me explain. I don't trust anyone, not even these niggas standing beside me. But I trust them more than my own flesh and blood. Now, let me tell you a little secret." The dreadhead moved in closer. Marcus could smell cigarettes and alcohol wafting off his breath. "E-B-O. Everybody's an opp, which means everyone could get it."

Marcus gripped the blade in his pocket even tighter. Thumb pushing downwards.

"People can rep what they like, but there's way too many mogs in this city and I can smell one from a mile away. You ain't no Folk." The dreadhead spit on the ground and took another hit. Smoke spilled out his lips like a dragon.

Marcus looked up at the darkening sky. He felt fucked.

"Where's your slick rebuttal now? The clock's ticking, nigga."

Licking his gums, Marcus tried to remember what the hell the Folk's motto was. He could tell a few guys were becoming impatient in the back, bored and antsy to pop off.

All is something...

Marcus scratched his head, wishing he could snap his fingers and fade away. He thought about texting Gordo, but he knew that nigga was probably still at the car shop. The only way *out* was *through*.

He shoved the chubby nigga aside and bolted down the sidewalk.

Someone cursed him, and the sound of squeaky soles smacked against the concrete in the distance.

Here we go.

Marcus dared to glance behind him, and saw the dreadhead and the beanie nigga on his ass.

The dreadhead locked eyes with Marcus and grinned.

Marcus picked up the pace, skirting around a corner and sprinted towards a black fence. He hopped it, landing in the wet grass awkwardly. Something popped in his upper back.

The minutes were ticking. Marcus got up with a quickness and moved forward. Strands of grass caught in his wake.

Pushing globs of space between him and the GD, Marcus thought back to his brief stint running track and field in high school. His coach encouraged him to stick with the sport, pitching the possibility of a full-ride scholarship. It was a nice gesture, but he knew that shit wasn't going to make him any money and the thrill of winning wore off quickly. Medals didn't pay the bills.

Something whistled past Marcus' pointed ears and his eardrums popped. His heart beat like a titanium drum, the sound filling his headspace. Niggas were packing heat.

He lifted himself over another fence and swung his legs around, softly dropping down in the grass. His side ached something bad. A cramp was forming. Still, he couldn't let up.

A dog barked a couple yards over. Marcus could hardly see the Rottweiler in the darkness. It pulled at its steel chain leash, straining to escape the confines. White canines flashed in the darkness.

Marcus hated dogs, but he was more concerned with the dreadhead and the nigga with the beanie. The blunt seemed to have no effect whatsoever on their dogged speed.

His lungs burned. He simultaneously cursed the swishers in his pocket and his Uncle for introducing him to the art of smoking. He hurdled over a kiddie pool, catching a glimpse of his murky reflection surrounded by a halo of dead leaves.

An older black woman sat on the back porch in a rocking chair, oblivious to the chase going on in her own backyard. Probably deaf or blind. Or even worse, she was used to the bullshit; she chalked it up to just another day in the Chi.

Marcus knew he fucked up the moment he focused on the old lady. Valuable time wasted. Large hands gripped his shoulders and shoved him to the ground face-first. The smell of raw earth invaded his nostrils, and he spit out a mouthful of dead grass and a tangle of weeds. He lifted his head a couple of inches from the ground. Hot breath washed over his neck and the hairs bristled.

"Fu-fu nigga. Thought you could get away huh?"

The beanie nigga kicked Marcus in the side and he cringed. "We crack Stones like eggs. Feel me?"

"I'm not a Stone," Marcus' nose started to bleed.

"What I tell you about lies?" the dreadhead said. "Just keep on lying and see what happens."

The old lady made her way over, sticking her cane out, yelling in her raspy voice. Marcus couldn't tell if she was brave, dumb, or an angel in disguise. Either way he was thankful for the brief distraction.

"Get out my yard."

The dreadhead pulled his gun out of his waistband and pointed it at the old lady. "You better mind your fuckin business and get back inside that house. Don't think about calling the cops or it's your ass. Ya hear me?"

She threw her hands up, shuffling back towards her house.

"That's what I thought, bitch."

Marcus lashed out at the dreadhead, sweeping his ankle. He buckled. The beanie nigga fell on top of Marcus and caught him with an elbow to the face.

The dreadhead rolled over and picked his gun back up. He sauntered over and pushed the beanie nigga aside.

"We're going to end this now."

Marcus look up at the shaft of the pistol, staring him down like a black hole ready to swallow his nineteen years of existence. His hands grew sweaty and blood streamed down his chin. Closing his eyes, he readied himself for the inevitable.

Police sirens wailed in the distance.

"Motherfucker."

Marcus opened his eyes and saw the dreadhead and his friend climbing the fence. He patted himself down and almost cried. He was so thankful to be alive and breathing.

Red and blue lights flashed off the house. Marcus rolled over and almost wished he had been shot when he saw the two cops approaching him. Handcuffs in hand.

Marcus put his hands behind his head and sighed.

3.
Crooked Country

Gordo received the call at one in the morning. He had been playing *Call of Duty*, busting these dusty niggas online, and stuffing his face with nachos.

He saw Marcus' name alongside a money bag emoji pop up on his phone. Balancing the controller, he leaned over, and slid his finger across the screen.

"Aye Ice, what's good?" He put the phone on speakermode and continued aiming his AK-47 at a pixelated character running across the screen. Stabbing a button repeatedly, he let off a flurry of shots.

"Gordo, I know you're busy, but I need your help."

Pop. Pop. Pop. Pop. Pop.

Gordo nearly choked on a nacho and swallowed the jagged pieces down his throat. Someone ran up behind Gordo's character and pistol-whipped him to death.

"Fuck, you got me killed," Gordo grabbed the pop sitting on his desk and gulped it down. "This better be important."

"I got locked up. Need you to bail me out."

"Shit, you alright, fam?"

"Yeah, I'll tell you what happened when you come through."

"Say no more. I'm on the way."

"Bet."

Gordo counted out five hundred dollars and passed them to the guy on the other side of the window. The man had salt and pepper hair, skin the consistency of baked dough, and a grim demeanor.

"Looks about right," the guy said. "Inmate 247 will be released shortly. Please sit in the waiting area."

"What about my receipt?"

"You don't need one."

"What the fuck, bro?"

"I'm not your bro. Now go sit your ass down in the waiting area before I pocket this cash and call security."

Gordo stormed off. He paced back and forth in the waiting area. He took off his fitted cap and fanned himself with it, wishing for some goddamn air.

How the hell was it so goddamn hot? The government can't even afford to pay for some AC. Makes no sense.

Gordo went into the restroom, searching for an open stall. He closed the door behind him and sat on the seat with his head cradled in his hands. He wiped the sweat off his forehead.

Marcus was probably locked up for some bullshit reason. Cops trying to hit quotas or taking out their pent-up aggression on the youth. He couldn't take this shit.

Feeling the anger swelling up inside his head, he punched the wall and the entire bathroom seemed to shake. The pressure inside his chest started to ease up, but his hand stung like he'd put it in a hornet's nest.

The dull fluorescent lights overhead seemed to intensify.

"Gotta get out of this fuckin' city," he muttered to himself.

Gordo threw some cold water on his face and shook it off. He stared at his reflection in the mirror, not sure what he was looking at. He exited the bathroom and saw Marcus looking around the waiting room.

"Ayo, Ice." Gordo waved him over.

Marcus came over and hugged Gordo.

"You have no idea how much I appreciate you, nigga."

"No issue. You know I got you."

"This nigga got stabbed right before you came through. That's why it took so long for them to let me out. Wanted to make sure I didn't instigate the situation."

"That's wild. What happened?"

"I don't know. I was keepin' to myself and then there was a bunch of yelling and shit. This nigga was holding his stomach. Blood everywhere. And get this, apparently the other nigga made a weapon out of his inhaler."

"Niggas get real inventive in here. Maybe in a parallel universe, that nigga's a scientist or something. The black Elon Musk."

"Yeah, it's crazy. And who knows? You might be right."

"Let's get the fuck outta here. This place gives me the chills."

Gordo listened to Marcus retell the night's events as he drove him home. He wished he could've been there to make sure he was alright.

"You should've brought some heat with you. I keep tellin you."

"Yeah, I know. I just hate carrying the shit on me. Imagine if the cops found a piece on me. Who knows when I'd get out."

"I hear you, but still...nigga almost blew your brains out. You got lucky."

"I know, I know."

"I know you know, but that's not enough. These niggas are reckless. They're just itching to pull a trigger. They'll do whatever to gain some clout in these streets."

Marcus nodded.

"Listen, I don't want to be hard on you. This shit is just crazy. I don't want to see anymore of my people get buried. I've already seen enough."

"I feel you."

Gordo pulled up to Marcus' crib. The lights were out.

Marcus took a deep breath.

"You'll be alright. Your mom's probably knocked out."

"Yeah, I need to move out. She's been stressin' the hell out of me."

"I keep telling you to move in with me."

"Naw, we need to move out of state. Maybe somewhere out west like Cali. I'm sure they have plenty of cars we could hit out there."

"Keep on dreamin and maybe we'll make it happen."

Marcus got out the car. "Maybe. And remind me to give you that bail money back on payday."

"Yeah, yeah." Gordo drove off into the night.

4.
Cheetah Piss

Sly cursed his key fob. This was the fifth time he pressed the button, and the car door was still locked. His neck felt tight, and the sun was beaming a little too loudly for his taste. Just when he was on the verge of saying fuck it, the lock clicked, and he was able to get in his car.

He cruised down the road and turned up the radio, allowing the bass to engulf him. Big Redd's song "Optics Freestyle" was playing. The low pitch in the beat seeped into every cell in his body and he nodded his head in sync with the hypnotic rhythm.

His rhythm was thrown off the moment a squeegee hit his windshield with a thud and slid across the glass in a horizontal line. A blurry brown face smirked behind the soapy water, wielding the squeegee like a black trophy.

Sly rolled his window down and could feel the tension building in his chest. The demons were calling. "Hey nigga, what the fuck are you doing?"

"I'm cleaning your windshield. Providing a necessary service. It was dirty."

"It's *my* car, nigga. If I want it to be dirty, it can be dirty. I own this shit. And who are you to deem it necessary?"

"I'm trying to make a living, my nigga. Why's that such an issue?"

The streetlight remained red, swaying in the wind. Sly tried reading the furrow lines in the squeegee man's weathered face.

"The fact that you even have to ask is pissing me off…"

"Listen my brother, I just want to clean your windshield and make some money. I need to eat."

Sly opened the car door and stepped out. "I'm sorry I have to do this, but you are not my brother. We share no blood, nigga."

The squeegee man pushed the squeegee out in front of him like a sword as he backed away.

"I don't want no smoke."

"It's too late for all that shit."

Sly snatched the squeegee and tossed it aside, moving forward. He clipped squeegee man with sloppy right hook. Blood gushed out of his nostrils as he fell backwards. Hands outstretched, pleading for him to stop.

Hovering over the squeegee man, Sly's anger poured out of every cell like gasoline. He felt like he was going to spontaneously combust. Cars honked behind him, and a few cruised around them. Middle fingers sailing in the air.

"Saved by the bell, nigga."

Sly massaged his jaw on the way home, weaving in and out of traffic like a speed demon. He managed to find a spot outside his apartment complex and parallel parked. It wasn't perfect but fuck it.

Who's going to check me?

He took the stairs to the third floor and fumbled with the keys, opening the door, and slamming it behind him as he sauntered into the kitchen, grabbing a pop out the fridge. He needed some caffeine in his system or something. Things like tea did nothing for him.

"Had a bad day, big bro?" his little sister Alana asked. She sat at the kitchen table surrounded by a stack of colored paper and a number of origami pieces in various forms of construction.

"How'd you know?"

"I'm your sister, nigga. I literally live with you. I can tell you're in a bad place. Want to talk about it? Healthy to get it out when it's fresh on your mind."

Sly popped the tab open and took a sip wondering how kids had an innate wisdom despite their age. "You know those squeegee niggas love running up on you. They don't even have the courtesy of *asking* if I need my windshield cleaned. They just do it with their hand out expecting something in return. The nerve... And then you got niggas out here reppin shit they have no right to be reppin. I mean the sheer lack of integrity bothers me on a core level."

"Damn, I feel you, but I mean we all gotta eat right?"

"You sound like the squeegee nigga," Sly grimaced. "Regardless, it's the principle."

"You didn't hurt anyone did you?"

Sly looked away, feeling the raw skin burn on his knuckles. He took another sip.

"I'm not God, Sly. I'm not judging you. I just don't want your anger to consume you. You're all I got."

Any remnants of anger instantly washed away and Sly felt his heart soften. He wiped away a tear and took another sip. "I'm working on it. Just know I love you."

"I know, but guess what? I got you a gift."

"What kind of gift?" Sly chugged the rest of the pop. So much was going on inside his stomach, he couldn't distinguish the emotions swimming inside from one another. They might as well have been sharks trying to swallow him whole.

"Hold on a sec."

Sly watched her disappear into her room and she returned, grinning with her hands behind her back.

"What is it Lana?"

She pulled her hands out, revealing a cylindrical container the size of his middle finger.

"Cheetah Piss."

"Cheetah Piss! How the hell did you get this? You're only sixteen."

"It's a secret. Either way, I had a feeling you would need it."

"You smoking weed? Be honest."

"Naw, this is a gift for you and only you."

Sly squeezed the sides of the container and it popped open. He fished the pre-roll out the case and smelled the heady aroma. "Oh this is gonna hit. I can tell."

Without hesitation, Sly leaned over and gave Alana a bear hug, squeezing her small frame in his arms. She smelled like coconut shampoo.

"I can't breathe."

"Sorry about that. Just wanted to tell you thank you. Really needed this."

Sly cracked a window in the kitchen, pulled a lighter out of his pocket, and pulled on the joint. He blew out a plume of smoke that coiled around his head like a snake.

The tension in his muscles loosened, and he sank into the couch like jelly. He thought back to the bag of money in the car, thinking about all the things he could do with that cash. Only problem is it didn't belong to him.

He took another pull and coughed, playing with the white paper crane in his free hand. One of the wings ripped.

"Fuck."

5.
Westside Bound

"Marcus, is that you?" His mom's soft voice flowed out of the filmy darkness like a blood orange rose.

"Yeah."

"What are you doing coming home at this ungodly hour?"

"Ran into some complications."

"Complications huh? Did you manage to grab the milk like I asked?"

"Naw, I forgot. I'll grab it in the morning."

"It might as well be the morning."

Marcus looked at the clock in the kitchen. The glowing numbers read 4:44 AM.

His mom looked exhausted. Probably stayed up all night waiting for him. Guilt welled up in his throat, threatening to spill down his chest.

"What happened to your face?" She went to touch his cheek.

He recoiled. "Please mom. Don't touch me."

Her bottom lip trembled. It had been doing that a lot lately.

Marcus wanted to ask her about it, tell her she should see a doctor with a gentle nudge, but he didn't want to worry her, especially at this hour.

"Who hurt you? Do you need me to call your uncle?"

"I'll be alright. Just a scratch."

"Looks like more than that, Marcus. Don't be getting into fights now. I worry bout you."

Marcus went into the bathroom and switched on the light. The bare lightbulb flickered, struggling to come to life. He grabbed a red rag from the cabinet and wiped the cut on his left cheek. Moving in closer to get a better view of his face, he assessed the damage. A couple nasty bruises around his nose and the cut.

Not too bad, he thought.

The pain would pass with time and maybe some alcohol.

A hairline crack ran down the left-hand side of the mirror, dividing Marcus' face into multiplicities. It made him dizzy and nauseous.

"All is one," he said, remembering the motto he had forgotten earlier.

"All is one," his thousand-faced reflection lip-synched the words.

Marcus poured some Actavis into a red Solo cup and mixed it with some pineapple-flavored pop. He watched it bubble. He stirred it with a silver butter knife while watching the pretty Korean anchor drone on TV about the failing healthcare system.

The video camera shifted to a birds-eye view of the Wild 100's, hovering over the notorious neighborhood. The camera floated right above desolate streets, empty lots, and burnt-out buildings. It resembled a third-world country, an urban warzone.

"This is the scene where an unidentified man let off shots on the Southside of Chicago on a beautiful Fourth of July weekend. Four people were injured and two confirmed dead. Police are still investigating the crime and suspects are still on the loose."

Marcus turned up the volume a few notches and took a sip.

"This weekend alone, fourteen people were caught up in the heartless shootings..."

Marcus took a generous sip and absentmindedly rubbed his jaw. He wondered if he knew any of the people who'd been shot. He was still waiting to hear about funeral arrangements for Lucas. He took another sip, this time letting the cup stay tilted upward for much longer than usual.

Wiping away a lone tear, Marcus guzzled down the rest of the lean. He didn't want to feel a damn thing. He laid down on the bed and stared up at the ceiling. A warm buzz nestled inside the crown of his head and trickled downward into his jaw, taking away the pain.

The sun nearly blinded Marcus as he stepped outside. An assortment of tools clanged against one another inside the bag hanging from his shoulder.

Gordo's '97 Chevy Cavalier, also known as Green Ivy,

sat idling on the curb. King Louie blasted out the speakers, reverberating off the windshield. Rocking a bucket hat with a floral design, Gordo stuck his thick neck out the window.

"Hurry up, nigga." Gordo looked at the imaginary watch on his wrist and feigned concern.

Marcus tossed the duffel bag into the backseat and slid into the passenger side, kicking aside empty fast-food bags and discarded cigarette boxes. They dapped hands and Gordo's eyebrows rose once he got a really good look at his friend.

"The fuck happened to your face?"

"Nigga I told you what happened. Why you actin' brand new all of a sudden?"

"It was dark outside. I didn't really get a chance to get a good look at your face. They really fucked you up, boi."

Marcus rolled down the window. He needed some air.

"Don't be like that, nigga. I'm just saying that knife of yours ain't good for nothin."

"Alright nigga. I brought the piece with me."

Marcus pulled out his Beretta M9 handgun and enjoyed the weight of it. He felt like he could take God out with this baby in his hand.

Gordo grinned, flashing his teeth.

"Looks like you're starting to smarten up, nigga. You should've brought that with you last night and let those shots off like-" he pointed his finger at the stop sign, "YOP YOP YOP."

Marcus laughed. He put the gun back in the bag, folding it up in a black shirt.

"For real though. How are you going to pull any pussy with that face of yours?"

"Damn nigga, you won't let me live, will you?"

Gordo laughed, turning up the music in the car. He pulled out a black and mild, keeping one hand on the wheel. He slid it between his lips and lit it. The cherry burned bright red. He took a puff and passed it to Marcus.

"Where are we going?" Marcus took a long drag.

"The Westside."

"Alright." He passed the black back to Gordo.

WGCI 107.5 finished out a song by Saba, and transitioned into smooth R&B. Marcus nodded along to the soulful voices streaming out the speakers until they became distorted and fizzled out completely.

"Damn Gordo, when you gonna get this radio fixed? I mean you work at an auto shop."

"The nigga who works in electronics is a weirdo and he acts sheisty. I don't want him touching my baby."

"Where your aux cord at?"

"Left it at home. Just change the station."

"Why don't you just get it fixed somewhere else? I know you got the money."

"Seems like a waste of paper."

"Really?"

"I'm saving up, my nigga."

"For what?"

"A way out."

6.
Finesser Studebaker

Marcus played with a deck of cards. He failed to shuffle them correctly and they slid out his small hands. He recollected the reds and blacks and shoved them back together. Despite his butter fingers, he continued shuffling. The cards smacked against each other and reminded Marcus of his stepdad's firm hand. He shivered.

Smack. Smack. Smack.

Marcus admired the well-dressed magicians on TV, enthralled by the tricks on the screen. He worked hard to mimic their hand movements and body language. They were flawless in their execution and delivery.

Uncle Jimmy flipped through today's newspaper. It was part of his midday routine, especially now that he was out of a job.

"Why do you steal?" Marcus asked. He instantly regretted the question, wishing he could swallow the words back up. His eyes were fixated on his uncle's hands and specifically his leather belt.

Jimmy looked up from the *Chicago Tribune* and wiped his nose with the bottom of his wrist. "I don't think of it as stealing. I just take things."

"Isn't it bad though? The Bible said something about not stealing. What if you go to hell? It's hot down there, and scary."

He turned another page. "Sounds like we need to have a bit of a man-to-man discussion. You feel like you can handle that, lil nigga?"

Marcus nodded.

"Don't tell your mom now. She'll have my ass. Pinky promise."

Marcus curled his pinky finger around his uncle's. "Cross my heart and hope to die."

"No one asked you to do all that, but it'll do. Pull up a chair."

Marcus did as instructed and got comfortable in a big chair.

"The Bible's got a lot of good things in it, but the people who use it are something else. You know Reverend Arthur isn't the most perfect man. Shit, the man's cheating on his wife with a couple of the girls who sing in choir."

Marcus' eyes grew wide and his mouth formed an O. "Really?"

"Yeah, really. I know it's hard to believe, especially when he gets up there every Sunday wiping the sweat off his shiny ass forehead and preaching up a storm. Let's just say when you learn the rules, there's certain ways to get around them. Make em work for you."

42

A few cards flew out of Marcus' hands. He carefully slid the cards back into the deck, staring at the small hole in the five of hearts he held.

"You see these shoes?"

Marcus appraised the fresh black and white Nikes on his uncle's big feet. He never saw them before. They were clean, slick and *whole*. As far as Marcus knew, his uncle only owned a pair of boots and some Adidas kicks that were missing a stripe.

"Wow. Those are nice. When'd you get em?"

"Couple days ago. The Adidas were fallin' apart. Figured I'd go out and get me a new pair. I walked in the shoe store a few blocks over, tried on a few different pairs and chose these."

Marcus stared at his uncle's shoes. Thoroughly impressed.

"What did you do with the old ones?"

"Put em in the box. Thought someone else might like them."

"That's cool. So it was like a trade?"

Uncle Jimmy nodded. "Yeah something like that. Just remember everything comes with a price."

"And no one stopped you?"

"Nope. How could they?"

"I mean..."

"I know what you mean. But there's a trick to taking something. You have to be smooth. You have to pull it off with a certain amount of flair and *finesse*. You see those magicians on TV? They have the keys to life."

Marcus nodded, struggling to pronounce *finesse*. Later, it became one of his favorite words.

* * *

Working in the sweltering heat of the basement, Marcus struggled to keep up. He pinched his sweat drenched t-shirt right beneath the collar. Teasing it back and forth, he felt a wave of cool air travel down his neck and upper chest.

He stared at the clock. The hands seemed to have hardly moved since the last time he looked.

Only an hour left in this bitch and I'm home free.

Marcus pushed the cart of bedsheets forward. He stopped and popped open the door on the industrial-sized washing machine. With slick hands, he gathered up a pile of white sheets, wondering what kind of nasty shit he was coming into contact with. Ignoring the possibilities, he shoved the ball of sheets inside.

He wiped his forehead off with the bottom of his work t-shirt. He walked over to the next washer and pushed another pile of musty sheets into the void. Slamming the door shut, he adjusted the knobs and pressed start. The sheets started to spin in a cycle of spiraling white. He stared at his tired reflection melting into a soft metallic blaze.

Marcus was the darkest person working in the basement and had been since he first nailed the job. His co-workers were brown too, but multiple shades lighter than him. They moved back and forth carrying baskets full of sheets and towels.

An older Spanish woman by the name of Cristina, who always wore a blue bandana, fanned herself with a magazine.

"Tengo calor," she said to no one in particular.

Cristina had always been sweet, even going so far as to bring him Spanish dishes on occasion.

"You alright?" Marcus asked, genuinely concerned. She probably needed a break, or maybe even a vacation. The heat was stifling and taking a toll on everyone.

"Si si, Marcus." She smiled warmly.

"Don't work too hard, Cristina. I worry about you."

"Thank you, Marcus."

Marcus moved onto a cart of wet towels, waiting for the dryer. He wondered whose lazy ass left these for him. Biting his tongue, he stuffed the towels into the open space.

Somehow, it reminded him of Gordo. They met early in high school, a bond forged by breaking the rules and giving the middle finger to authority. However, the thing that appealed to Marcus the most was Gordo's skills. He had a knack for taking things apart. A keen eye for disassembling objects and distilling them down to their core components. That was valuable.

Marcus always thought of himself as a solo finesser. It made things easier. Less dangerous, and he kept 100 percent of the profit. Except he wished he could share some of stains he hit. Point out the poor unsuspecting mogs he jacked week in and week out.

It had been a hot minute since they hit a lick, and Marcus was itching to get back to the *real* work. It had been far too long and his pockets were beginning to hurt.

Pulling his phone out his jeans, he thumbed the crack running over the camera. *Need to get that fixed one of these days,* he thought. *Matter of fact, I just need to get a new phone.*

He chilled in the corner of the basement, played a few games, checked his texts and wondered why his phone was so dry. No one hit his line. He usually had a couple people blowing him up, and Gordo always sent him a few texts checking on him.

The washers continued to spin and shake in the background.

Marcus' phone vibrated and a text notification popped up. He entered his code and slid his thumb down the screen.

"You ready? I got some work on deck."

"Been ready."

Marcus clocked out of work and changed into a normal set of clothes. It felt good to get rid of the weight of the day and shove it inside his duffle bag. A shower would be nice, but that could wait.

He walked outside and took a deep breath, relishing the breeze running across his glistening brown skin. A car sped past and Marcus waited to cross the street.

A bright light reflected off the bus station's glass window, emphasizing the woman sitting on the bench below it. She had mocha chocolate colored skin, long curly hair, full lips, and freckles that seemed ready to leap off her face. Her eyes hidden behind sunglasses were buried deep in a book.

Marcus struggled to read the title.

Must be smart, he thought.

He jogged across the street. Normally, he took the train, but it looked like he'd be taking the bus home today.

Marcus didn't want to be a creep, so he scrolled through his phone until the bus pulled up. He looked at the bench and didn't even notice her getting up. She was already entering the bus.

He ran up the steps and paid in cash before taking a seat beside her. The doors closed and the bus took off.

The woman stared outside the window at the passing cars.

Marcus usually had a few slick lines ready to go, but he felt his heart lodged in his throat. He didn't know what it was about this girl, but she was like some distant planet drawing him into her orbit.

"Excuse me..." he said.

She turned towards him, and the light shining behind her seemed to radiate off her in waves. It was almost overwhelming.

"What book were you reading outside?"

"*Black Gypsies.* It's a poetry collection by this guy named Apollo Jones. I'm pretty sure it's a pseudonym, but the poetry inside is breathtaking."

"That's cool. I like poetry. I'm more of a Saul Williams fan myself. Maybe I can borrow it sometime?"

"I mean I just met you," she adjusted her sunglasses. "Don't get ahead of yourself. Poetry is close to my heart and I share it with those I love."

"I'm sorry. My name's Marcus. People call me Ice."

"Ice? Like Iceberg Slim? I hope you're not a pimp or anything, cuz I'm not the one." She clutched the book to her chest.

"Naw, naw. I'm no pimp. Forget the nickname. You can just call me Marcus."

"Okay Marcus, my name's Zoe. I like Marcus much better than Ice. You can call me Zoe."

"Like Zoe Kravitz?"

Zoe rolled her eyes. "Yes, like Zoe Kravitz. You think that girl's pretty?"

"She's cute, but I think she needs to eat a little more."

"I think she's overrated. She tries too hard to be different and edgy and her band is trash in all caps."

"Damn, you two got beef?"

"Naw, she just rubs me the wrong way."

"I feel you."

"So what do you do Marcus?"

"What do I do? Well..."

"Hol up, looks like this is my stop."

Marcus looked outside and realized they were in Oak Park. Ole girl has a little money in her family, or maybe she was just showing off. Either way, Marcus' interest was thoroughly piqued.

She got up and Marcus let her out of the seat. "Before you go, could I get your number? I'd love to take you out sometime."

Zoe smiled, took out a pen and scribbled her phone number on the back of a fortune cookie paper. "Have a good day, Marcus."

"You too," he said, turning the piece of paper over to read the fortune on the other side.

7.
Sun Goddess

Zoe smelled her armpits, making sure the summer heat didn't betray her. Her citrus deodorant wafted off her in waves. She continued walking towards her apartment, thinking about Marcus. He was cute and had a disarming allure about him.

Don't get ahead of yourself, Zoe thought. *He's just another nigga trying to get in your pants...you don't even know his birth chart. Could be a Libra for all you know.*

It had been a couple years since her last relationship with a Gemini man. He was charming at first, but that wore off over time. She wished men would come with a label because this nigga was the textbook definition of toxic. He was out of his fucking mind. Didn't know what career he wanted to pursue, let alone what he wanted in a "relationship." She did a lot of inner work in the meantime, healing her heart with therapy, reiki, and a strict gym routine.

Still, she thought it would be nice to have a partner in her life as she unlocked the door. Someone she could lean on, confide in and cuddle with on lonely nights.

She considered texting Marcus, but felt like it was way too soon. Didn't want to come across as thirsty. Fear welled up in her stomach and she took a few deep breaths, soothing her nervous system. She decided to wait, and see if he would actually follow through.

My time is valuable. My time is sacred.

She washed her face and went into her bedroom, searching for her bag. Fishing around the compartments, she pulled out a brand-new top from Victoria Secret. She tried it on in front of her mirror, turning from side to side and snapping a couple pics.

Can't believe I was able to pull this off.

She'd strolled into the store, whipped out her magnet and slid the security tag off like it was nothing. One of store associates waved to her and told her to have a nice day as she exited the store. She considered going back for seconds, but her OG always taught her not to be greedy and to keep her ego in check. That's how you get out clean. The sage advice brought her a long way and kept her from getting caught up with the law.

Zoe put the top away and went to the corner of her room where her altar was situated. She drew the blinds and grabbed a torch lighter. Her altar was small, but she was proud of it. Bay leaves, labradorite, smoky quartz, and black tourmaline surrounded three 7-day candles waiting to be lit along with a picture of her cousin Lucas, grinning. Tears streamed down her face, ruining her makeup, and she sniffled, missing him. Wishing she could hear his goofy laugh again.

She remembered getting the call from her friend at the

tattoo shop. She left Starbucks and nearly spilled her drink while crossing the street. The world around her was sucked up into a vacuum of pure shock and pain.

Lighting the candles, she felt a wave of relief and comfort wash over her. She closed her eyes and tried connecting with her ancestors, searching for their energy. A warm presence slowly filled the room, almost cupping her heart. The candles' flames flickered, giving her the confirmation she was seeking.

She silently asked for protection and safe passage to the other side for Lucas. Gratitude permeated her heart, and she mouthed the words *thank you.*

Her phone vibrated and she wiped her eyes, checking her phone.

It was Marcus.

8.
Party Monster

Gordo struggled to button his white pants around his waist, but they fit. *Barely.* He kept reminding himself to hit the gym, but he had a genuine belief that there was a hidden power in his stomach. 'Fat niggas do it better' was his go to phrase.

The squad was going to hit a house party tonight, and he wanted to try something different. He was known for taking certain fashion risks. Most were hit or miss, but it was something he enjoyed. Whenever he stepped out, the reactions were priceless.

"White pants?" Marcus asked.

Gordo looked down at his white pants and didn't see any smudges or stains. They were flawless.

"Nigga, these pants are dope. You must be lowkey jealous or somethin because these will pull. Bitches. They're like a magnet."

"They're an accident waiting to happen. What if someone spills their drink. Whatchu gonna do then?"

"Damn, I didn't think that far. I'll just be careful, nigga.

How hard could that be? Niggas used to rock white pants in the 70's all the time."

"One problem. This ain't the 70's though."

Jordan Hooper walked over and put his arm on Gordo's shoulder. "As long as they pull thots, I support you."

"Thots, thotties, bitches, it really doesn't matter. As long as they have a cute smile and a nice ass I'll be happy."

"And know how to cook." Jordan snickered.

"Can't be mad at that. Remember when that girl Bri cooked me some french toast after we had fucked? It was fire," Gordo said, reminiscing. They went outside, taking in the cool air.

"The sex or the french toast?"

"Both."

"Who the hell are we waiting on?" Gordo said, growing impatient. He checked his phone. It was still early, but he didn't like sitting around for too long. It made him anxious and he wanted to show off these pants and get a drink in his system.

"We're waiting on Key," Jordan said.

Gordo let out a dramatic sigh, smacking the hood of the car. "On God, if that nigga doesn't show up in the next five minutes..."

"In the meantime, I'll just light one while we're waiting," Marcus said. He fished out a pre-rolled joint from the car's front console. He couldn't find his lighter.

"Anyone got a light?" Marcus asked as he triple-checked his pockets, patting them down. "Where the fuck..."

"Hol up." Jordan fished a lighter out of a pocket inside his black jacket and tossed it to Marcus. "Heads up."

Marcus caught the Bic in his hand. He placed the joint in his mouth and tried to light it, but the wind continuously blew out the flame. Cursing, he cupped his hands around the tip as he lit up. He took a deep inhale and released the smoke through his nostrils.

"Stop being greedy, nigga. Let me get a hit." Jordan reached his hand out and Marcus shot him a crazy look.

"Hold on, nigga. The joint's not gonna disappear."

"Nigga, I gave you the lighter. That gives me the automatic *right* of having one of the first puffs."

Gordo leaned against the driver's side of his car and scrolled through his phone. Nothing new or exciting going online. It was a matter of habit. Almost as bad as his food addiction, but this craving could instantly be assuaged with a few clicks. It was too easy.

I need to quit checking this shit every five minutes, he thought. *Be better off looking for new targets. God knows I could use the money.*

Key pulled up on a black bike too small for his tall frame. He stood up as he pedaled forward, leaning his weight on the handlebars.

"Nigga, if you don't get your tall ass off that bike," Jordan said.

Key hopped off his bike and hid it in the bushes. It was almost as if it was never there to begin with.

"I told y'all I'd be late," Key said. "Bet the party hasn't even started to get poppin yet."

"Bad and boujee lookin ass nigga," Jordan said.

"I can't afford a new pair of shoes lookin ass nigga," Key said.

"At least I take care of my shoes and don't ride around on a bike lookin ass nigga."

"Alright nigga. You win."

Gordo started up the car and waited for everyone to hop inside. He couldn't wait to hit this party. He couldn't remember the last time he'd been this excited. Maybe it really was something about the white pants.

Marcus turned up the volume. Hurt Everybody's song "Social Network" was playing through the aux cord.

I brought all my homies, who's going to stop us now…

Everyone nodded their heads to the song in unison mouthing the word *gang, gang, gang, gang*. The car shook and the bass sounded like a kaiju monster in the trunk.

The party was lit. Cars spilled out of the driveway and wrapped around the block by the time Gordo passed by the house.

"Ain't that some shit," Key said, taking a hit of the joint in the backseat.

"We can walk," Marcus said.

"I don't know bout you, but you can drop me off right here," Key said.

"Nigga if you don't sit your jiffy peanut butter looking ass back down," Jordan said, pulling him back in the car.

"I'm sure I can find some parking on the next block over."

After a few minutes, Gordo parallel parked into a tight spot and everyone got out.

"This party must be bangin," Gordo said. He was surprised

the cops hadn't been called. The music was loud as fuck and they couldn't even see the house from here.

"I got some pills in case y'all want to get right," Key said, shaking a small clear baggie. Blue pills shook inside.

"Nigga, don't tell me you're already rollin," Gordo said.

"Bitch I might be."

Gordo passed on the offer and so did Marcus. Jordan grabbed one and popped it on the spot.

They walked up to the two-story house. A few niggas were outside smoking while a couple of cute girls were booed up with men in the shadows.

"There better not be a bunch of niggas here," Gordo said.

"It's all good. I assure you there's gonna be some hoes," Key said.

Gordo side-eyed Key. He was a good friend, but not always one to keep his word.

"Follow me."

Key led the way inside and dapped up a few people.

Gordo surveyed the scene, checking out more than a few cute girls who looked just right. He caught a few eyes checking out his pants. It could've been for better or worse, but he took it as a compliment nonetheless.

"Where's the drink at?" Jordan asked.

"In the kitchen," Key said.

Gordo made his way to the kitchen, weaving his way through a number of sweaty bodies. Pheromones and liquor filled the atmosphere - a heady mix.

Marcus started pouring up drinks for the crew. Dark liquor

and pop. He had a penchant for mixing things just right.

A well-dressed nigga with designer frames and a bald head walked up and hugged Key. Gordo squinted at the newcomer. Something felt off about him.

"Glad you could make it, fam."

"You know I had to come through. Let me introduce you to my niggas."

"This is Marcus, Gordo, and Jordan. No relation to Michael."

"This nigga," Jordan said. "Always got jokes."

"Nice to meet you all. I'm Octavius, but everyone just calls me 'O.' If you need anything, just ask. I'll be floating through the party."

"You got a nice place," Marcus said.

O took off his Tom Ford glasses and wiped off the lens with a red cloth.

"I appreciate it, my nigga. I worked hard to get here."

"I can tell," Gordo said.

"Alright, have a good time." He waved as he walked off.

Once O was out of earshot, Jordan cleared his throat. "That nigga looks like a lame with money."

"That lame gives me these pills, nigga. So he's good in my book."

"I don't care. Something about him rubs me the wrong way," Jordan said.

"He's a nice guy. I don't see the problem," Key said.

"It's a gut thing, nigga. Intuition," Jordan said. "I'm telling you…I got a bad feeling about this nigga."

"Yeah I can see what you're sayin," Gordo said, handing out drinks and rubbing his gut.

Marcus had enough of the small talk. "Aye niggas, fuck all the bullshit. Let's get this shit rollin."

They raised their drinks and Gordo took his straight to the head, gulping the dark liquid down his throat. Satisfied, he poured himself another.

Six drinks later, Gordo was in the living room, dancing to The Weeknd's "Party Monster." He swayed from side to side.

"I'm good, I'm good, I'm great. No it's been a while, now I'm mixing up the drink," he sang along with The Weeknd.

Gordo didn't really know how to dance, but he faked it. He shimmied from side to side, targeting a dark-skinned girl with ample curves. He danced his way over to her and she bent over, grabbing her ankles, and started twerking. Her ass cheeks shook like an earthquake and nearly spilled out of the bottom of her short dress.

"Oh gawd," Gordo said in amazement, moving closer.

They made eye contact and Gordo knew it was a go. He grabbed her ass, wrapped his hands around her waist and pulled her in closer. He had a hard-on and rubbed it against her ass, growing even harder.

She turned around and pushed him onto the couch. Gordo took another sip of his drink, and readied himself for what was to come.

"Relax," she said.

She eased his legs open, turned around and bent over so Gordo could see her ass in all of its glory. He wiped the sweat off his face, hoping he'd remember this in the morning.

Gordo closed his eyes, enjoying the lap dance for all it was worth. Her firm ass grinded against the hard-on throbbing in his white pants. He grinned, thinking *this is what heaven must feel like, or something close.*

Someone bumped into the couch and Gordo's drink flew out his hand, spilling on the twerking girl and his pants.

"What the fuck, nigga?" The girl stood up wiping her hands on her purple dress. "You ruined my dress."

"My bad."

Gordo was in a complete daze, surprised by the sudden turn of events. His empty cup dangled from his hand and his hard-on was completely gone. What a waste.

"Way to ruin a good moment, nigga. I was thinking about fuckin your fat ass too." She walked off, searching for the bathroom and some paper towels.

Gordo slumped down into the folds of the couch, dumbfounded. He lost some potential pussy and his pants were beyond fucked. He wished he could snap his fingers and disappear, but that wasn't an option.

"Damn nigga, what happened to your pants?" Key said.

"Long story," Gordo said, grabbing some napkins. He dabbed at the dark stain, attempting to soak up the wetness.

"Where's Marcus at?" Gordo asked.

Key pointed behind the couch and Gordo turned around.

Marcus was dancing with a petite girl in the middle of the crowd. It was almost as if a spotlight was placed directly overhead of them. The girl wore a blue dress that hugged her curves and revealed her back. Japanese characters ran down her spine, disappearing into the V of Marcus' hands.

They began making out, and Gordo sobered up a little bit.

"Ice might be getting some booty tonight," Gordo said, slightly jealous.

"Aye don't sleep. Ice got some moves," Jordan chimed in, sitting down next to Gordo on the couch. He threw back the rest of his drink.

The song changed to Rae Sremmurd's "No Type" and the crowd went wild. Marcus and his mystery girl were swallowed up by the hype crowd.

Jordan and Key joined the crowd and Gordo slowly stood up.

"Fuck these pants," he said, moving onto the dancefloor.

Gordo caught Marcus glancing his way and gave him a subtle head nod. *At least my boy's about to pull some pussy tonight,* he thought. *He wins, we all win.*

O came through the crowd like a snake, easing his way around people on the dancefloor. He said *excuse me* and *sorry* multiple times before shouldering past Marcus with an extra umph.

Marcus turned around and shoved O. "What the fuck nigga? Couldn't you say excuse me? I don't give a damn if you own this place or not. Have some manners, uppity bitch."

O looked unfazed and simply dusted off his outfit. "I'm sorry you feel that way. Maybe you didn't hear me as I passed by."

A small crowd started to form around O, Marcus, and the mystery girl.

61

Key moved into the mix, wedging his way in between the two of them. "Aye hol up hol up, I'm here to maintain the peace. I can't have my niggas fightin."

"I wasn't fighting at all. I think your friend just had a little too much to drink. I strongly encourage you to look after your *friend* here. Things could get out of hand."

O adjusted his glasses and glared at Marcus for the briefest second.

Gordo had his hand on his piece, ready to pull it out of his stretch waistband if necessary. He was faded, but could still pull a trigger good as anyone. He was just itching to unload his anger on someone tonight.

Marcus told Zoe to hold on a second and moved towards Gordo, ready to stop the freight train coming this way.

"Is that nerdy-lookin nigga causing problems Ice? I'd fuck a nigga up."

"It's all good Gordo. I got it under control. And you don't need to be waving the piece around in here. Nigga shoved me and I'm handling it."

"Looks like it," Gordo said, crossing his arms.

Zoe came over and grabbed Marcus' wrist, leaning her body weight against his. She was shaking. "Let's get out of here. I can't stand bad vibes."

"Alright babe. Let's dip."

"Nigga's lucky..." Gordo said, letting his anger ease back down.

They left the party and Gordo looked back through the crowd, locking eyes with O, who was smirking.

9.
Gravitational Pools

Zoe stumbled into the hotel room and threw her purse on the carpet. Marcus pushed her against the wall and kissed her passionately. She felt his tongue slip inside her mouth and smelled the alcohol wafting off him.

"Hey…can you slow down a second?"

Marcus pulled back, lust dripping off him. "Yeah, you okay?"

"Yeah, I just don't want to make a mistake or move too fast," she felt the alcohol coursing through her body. The room was warm, and her perception was velvet soft. "I mean you're not even my boyfriend."

"That's fair. We can just chill."

"No, we're going to do some things…just don't overdo it," she gripped the hard-on in his jeans. "I'm tipsy."

Zoe started undoing his jeans and struggled to unlatch the belt.

"Hol up, I got it." She sat on the edge of the bed, watching him undo his pants. The silence had an electrifying tension and she was growing impatient. She pulled out her phone and threw on some Maxwell.

Marcus nearly fell on his ass as pulled his pants off his ankles. His throbbing dick poked through his boxers pointing at Zoe.

"Come over here before you bust your ass for real."

She kissed him and relished his firm hands moving over her body, exploring the slopes and curves like a cartographer exploring uncharted territory. Her body became even warmer as she grabbed his cock and took it inside her mouth. She played with the tip before taking it in more deeply.

Marcus moaned with pleasure.

Zoe hated sucking dick, but she really liked Marcus. The oral act felt like a chore, but she was in a giving mood. She pulled his dick out of her mouth and saliva ran down her chin, falling on the carpet in stringy loops.

Marcus pulled her to her feet and kissed her again before helping her out of her dress and tossing the bra and panties aside. She caught him staring in awe at her figure.

"You alright, Ice?" She grinned.

"Yeah…I mean…sorry," he said. "I knew your body would be nice, but this is something else."

"How would you describe it?" she asked, slowly moving towards him like a cobra.

"Fire," he said, staring the dark freckles on her naked body. She could feel how badly he wanted her and loved it.

We all can't be poets.

Zoe grabbed his wrist and pulled him towards the bed,

pushing him down on the comforter. She crawled on top of him, biting his neck softly, making sure to leave an imprint.

Marcus gripped fistfuls of cover and his face read nothing but ecstasy.

Zoe bent forward, raising her ass in the air as she readied herself for the main attraction. She slid his cock inside of her and gasped. She bit her lip as it filled her to the brim. Moving down, she was amazed at how it reached her innermost depths.

She rode Marcus, rubbing her hands through his hair, feeling the waves building up inside of her. She looked down at him, wondering how he could handle the raging monsoon inside her pussy.

Staring into his almond brown eyes, she bent over even further, laying chest to chest. She rubbed her small tits against his body as she slid up and down up and down up and down. He reached up and kissed her fully before rolling over, still inside her.

Marcus took the reins and raised her legs to the sky as he scooted closer. He entered her again and it was just as explosive as the first time, except now she was soaking wet. Gasping for air, she gripped the sheets as Marcus thrust inside her forcefully.

"You okay?" he asked, visibly concerned.

"I'm good."

He grinned and thrust inside her, bucking his hips with each movement. She felt a wave coming. It was small at first, but with each thrust it grew stronger and she could feel a tidal wave on the horizon.

Marcus' face took on a serious disposition, and it turned

her on even more. Zoe wrapped her legs around his back and pulled him in closer. He picked up the pace. She could feel the forceful impact of each thrust rock her body to the core.

Shaking, she wrapped her arms and legs around him even tighter, locking him in a cocoon of warmth and wetness. His thrusts slowed down, becoming more in tune with her waves, bringing her closer to that moment she yearned for. The moment calling her name.

He thrust three more times and with the last, he whispered in her ear, "I think I love you."

The wave came like a jolt of pleasure to her entire body. Eight thousand watts of bliss and sensual electricity surging through every cell of her being.

She melted inside of him, resting her head against his chest. He kissed her neck and dived underneath the sheets.

"I'm not finished yet."

She laughed.

Light came in the window, spilling across Zoe's face, clavicle, and breasts. The lower half of her body was wrapped up in sheets. Marcus lay next to her, lightly snoring.

She wrapped Marcus' gold cross around her finger. The chain grew taut, and she pulled him in for a deep kiss. Tongues lightly brushing against one another.

"What are you?" he said.

She paused and then her serene face twisted into scowl. "Nigga, I'm a woman. I'm stardust. I'm the universe distilled into flesh."

Marcus was taken aback. Visibly surprised by her sharp response.

Zoe was pretty sure it turned him on.

"I meant..."

"I know what you meant. You meant ethnicity, nigga. Think about how you phrase things. You know how many times people ask me that dumb ass question? It's ignorant as fuck."

"No, I'm sorry. I just-"

"It's okay. It gets me heated. Makes me feel like I'm less than human. Like I'm an animal or something."

Kissing her shoulder, Marcus wished he could melt her tension away with his touch alone. He wished he wasn't such a smart ass.

Zoe ran her fingers through her hair. "Since you asked, I'm half black, half gypsy."

"You lyin."

"Do I look like I'm lying?"

"No."

"My dad's black and my mother is Romani."

"Woah."

Twirling the cross back and forth, Zoe stared at the pores in Marcus' skin, searching for an entry point. Hoping she could be swallowed whole into the void.

"I think it's dope."

"Thanks." She rolled over and kissed him on the neck, loving the taste of his skin on her tongue. "You wanna know something funny?"

"Yeah."

"I got a theory. Most of our ancestors emigrated or were forced here one way or another. I think we're all gypsies at heart. Nomads. You know, travelers. Searching for a place to call home."

"I could see that," Marcus said.

Zoe released the cross from her hand and nuzzled into the crook of Marcus' neck, absorbing his warmth, and feeling his pulse beat through her. This moment felt absolutely divine, but she wondered how much longer she could hold onto this piece of time before it became a dim memory.

10.
Stain City

"Good things come to those who take," Gordo said, taking a pull of his blunt.

"Sounds like something my uncle would have said." Marcus waved the smoke out of his face.

"Sorry about that, nigga. Your uncle was a relatively smart man."

"He wouldn't be in and out of jail if he was that smart."

"Key word—*relatively.*" Gordo's round face was consumed by a cloud of marijuana smoke. "That's just part one of the Stain Scriptures."

"When will we hear part two?"

"When I figure it, nigga. No one was asking Bell Hooks, Aristotle or Dr. Umar Johnson when they're writing part two of their books or lectures. It's takes time to come up with these philosophies."

"On gawd, I feel you. You still planning to write a book one day?"

"You already know. It's percolating up here and down here."

Gordo pointed to his head and then pointed to his stomach. "And then it will spill out on the page."

There was a heavy knock on the window. Gordo almost dropped his blunt. He took a deep breath and rolled the window down to a set of grinning teeth. A couple were missing while the others were stained yellow.

"Fuck you want? You almost blew my high," Gordo said.

The missing teeth man held a squeegee in his left hand and clutched a bucket of dirty water in his other hand. His dark skin was tough as leather and freckles dotted his face like stars in a lost galaxy.

"Care to get your windshield cleaned?"

"Sure."

The squeegee man hurried to the front of the car and cleaned the window in a frantic fashion. With each pull of the squeegee, it emitted a sharp squeaky sound.

Gordo looked up at the red light, wondering how long they had been sitting there.

"That'll be 2 dollars, sir."

Gordo scrounged around his pockets and came up short.

"I got you." Marcus said, handing over a five-dollar bill to Gordo who transferred the money to squeegee man.

"Much appreciated." Squeegee man tipped an invisible hat and moved out of traffic's way as the light turned green and Gordo sped off.

"Who's that?" Gordo asked.

"Nobody," Marcus said, looking down at his phone.

"You can answer it."

"We're on a job."

"Right answer. You passed the test."

Marcus nodded, looking out the window.

Gordo and Marcus cruised underneath a gold-lettered sign proclaiming "Welcome to Chinatown." They passed a number of storefronts, banks, and restaurants with names veiled in Chinese symbols. The scent of Chinese food wafted inside the cracked window and Gordo's stomach grumbled.

"Might have to grab some fried rice and eggrolls on the way back," Gordo said.

"Good idea. We'll celebrate with some takeout."

"Look over there," Gordo said.

A black Dodge Charger with tinted windows and shimmering hubcaps parked on the side of the street. It looked mean. Gordo loved how smooth the engine sounded whenever he heard one pull up to the auto shop.

They parked down the road. Gordo scoped out the side street for any nosey fucks or cameras hidden in storefronts. No one seemed to be out. Still, he didn't like taking chances. Earlier that year, him and Marcus almost got caught stealing a Louis Vuitton bag some lady left resting against her groceries as she pulled money out the ATM five feet away. She turned around screaming and they dipped down the street, barely getting away.

Gordo looked down at his watch and his stomach grumbled. "Looks like it's about that time, nigga."

Marcus nodded and got out the passenger side. Popped the trunk. Gordo grabbed the car jack from the back. He moved

71

like a bear, eyes fixated on the Charger.

Getting down on his hands and knees, he inserted the car jack underneath the center of the car. He was overweight, but his heavy frame also gave him a distinct advantage over his co-workers when it came to moments like this. He cranked the jack with his forearm. Sweat dripped down his face as the car lifted off the ground.

"Now that's magic, baby," Gordo said.

"I see you," Marcus said.

"Grab the lug wrenches."

Marcus fished out two lug wrenches from the trunk and handed one to his partner. They removed the lug nuts from the wheels and admired how clean the hubcaps were.

"These are going to bring in some paper. Can't wait to hit the junkyard and get paid."

"All I see are dollar signs."

Gordo popped a hubcap off the rim and he set it aside carefully. He took a certain pride in disassembling a car. It gave him a sense of purpose. It was his own island of clarity. Zen. He tried meditating with a girl a couple years ago, but that couldn't calm his mind. The only thing that could achieve that was mechanic work. It was his form of active meditation.

They placed the hubcaps on top of flat cardboard boxes in Gordo's trunk and zipped them up in an oversized duffle bag.

"Ready to call it a day?" Gordo asked, growing sick and tired of this heat. It was September and 83 degrees. His fat ass couldn't handle it anymore.

"Yeah, let's get that Chinese food."

Gordo cruised down the street, eyeing the restaurants, trying to figure out which one would satisfy his hunger.

"Should we get shrimp broccoli or--"

Marcus interrupted, pointing to a Honda Civic "--STOP the car nigga. Stain alert."

"What the fuck are you talkin about..."

Gordo saw the Civic as they slowed down and noticed the driver's door wasn't shut properly. This happened once in a blue moon, but whenever it happened, Gordo thanked whoever was running things in the sky.

"Get out and I'll cruise around the block. Grab whatever you can, but be slick about it. I know you got the hands. I'll be back in two minutes flat."

"Bet."

Gordo watched Marcus get out and thought about handing him his piece, but decided to chill. Chinatown seemed deserted, and no one would say shit to Marcus.

Driving down the block, Gordo wondered how much money they'd be bringing in with their latest stain. The parts had to be worth a pretty penny, and might bring his savings to the next level.

Gordo dreamt of moving somewhere warm like Cali, Hawaii, or maybe even Panama. Maybe he'd be able to reconnect to his roots and really figure out what happened to his father once and for all.

He pulled up alongside the busted Civic and Marcus had a new duffle bag ready.

Marcus opened the passenger door and hopped inside with a huge grin on his face.

"Pull off nigga. We hit the motherload."

"What are you talking about?" Gordo said, growing antsy.

Marcus unzipped the big and opened it up and Gordo saw stacks of 100-dollar bills with thick rubber bands choking the money.

"Bands nigga. Bands," Marcus said, gripping a stack in his hand.

"Put that shit away. I'm getting stressed the fuck out just looking at it."

"Alright. Alright."

"You don't think it was anyone important we just jacked, do you?"

"Whoever has that whip ain't important. Just sayin."

"Maybe you're right. I just got this funny feeling in my stomach."

Gordo turned up the volume in his car, listening to the local radio play some Future.

God blessin all the trap niggas spilled out the speakers. Listening to Future's drugged out raps fill the interior of his ride, he wondered if Future was right. Maybe this was good karma paying off…finally.

A cool breeze drifted inside the car and Gordo shivered. He turned a corner and a siren went off. Blue and red lights reflected off Gordo's rearview mirror.

"Fuck, it's the cops," Gordo said. "Ain't that a bitch."

Marcus shot Gordo a stressed-out look, gesturing towards the bag of money in his lap.

"Throw it in the backseat. We're about to take a huge gamble."

Marcus put the bag in the back and wiped his sweaty hands on his jeans.

Gordo turned down the music, hoping his hunch would pay off. This is one of those times he had to put his faith into his gut and ride with it. Most of the time it worked in his favor.

Waiting for the cop to approach the car, Gordo reached into his pocket, rubbing the Panamanian Balboa coin for good luck. He needed every bit of it right now.

Gordo watched the cop saunter over to his window and stand with his hands on his hips. The cop was about 5'5, with shades, and a military haircut. He chewed on a mint obnoxiously. The smell made Gordo sick to his stomach.

"Good evening, could I see your license and registration?"

"Yeah, Marcus hand me the stuff out the glovebox."

"Do it slowly."

Gordo nearly balled up the registration in his hand before passing it to the cop. The cop took it and started looking through the documents, finger running across each line, and then stared at the license. He compared the face on the card to Gordo's.

"You gained a bit of weight, haven't you?"

Gordo gripped the steering wheel tightly, wishing he could rip it off and beat the cop to death with it. Instead, he took a deep breath and rubbed the coin in his pocket furiously, hoping it would absorb the anger swelling inside his chest.

"Looks like you're good to go. Either way, you should put that duffle bag to use and hit the gym more often."

Marcus leaned over, getting the cops attention. "Thanks, sir. Have a good day."

"You, too." The cop walked away, keys jingling by his side.

The cop got in his car, put the car into drive and slowly drove off.

"Fuck that nigga," Gordo said.

"We still got the money." Marcus said.

Gordo had completely forgotten. He looked in the backseat, almost amazed that the bag was still there.

"Oh shit, it worked."

"Hell yeah it worked."

"Looks like we'll be getting out the city sooner than later."

11.
Territorial Takeout

Licking the grease off his fingers, Sylvester "Sly" Jones pulled his car keys out of his pocket and pressed the button. No response.

"Jesus Christ. Just fuckin work for once."

He pressed it a couple more times until he saw the green light flash on his key fob.

Orlando Matthews sipped his drink and his eye peeked out from underneath his shades. "When are you getting that key fixed?"

"Soon. I just don't enough time in the day. You know how it is."

"Alright, my nigga." Orlando sipped on his drink obnoxiously.

Sly wiped his mouth and glanced out the window of the Chinese food joint. He almost choked when he noticed the nigga sitting in the passenger seat. The fake ass gangsta from the other day. The car's engine revved loudly as it pulled off.

Tires screeching.

"Where the fuck are they going?" Orlando asked.

"I think that's the nigga we almost killed last week."

"Think so? I couldn't even see his face. I just remember his pointy ears and weak ass lungs. He don't want no smoke."

"I don't forget faces," Sly pointed to his head and slammed a cash tip down on the table. "It's like a special talent of mine. Let's go."

Sly slid into the driver's side and started up the car. The engine roared and he took off. He glanced at the backseat and then he did a double-take.

"Aye where's the bag at? Did you move it?" Sly asked.

"Naw, I ain't move it. Is this a joke or something, because this really isn't the time."

Sly pulled the car over, tires screeching. He hopped out and popped the trunk. The bag was nowhere to be found.

"What the fuck, Sly?"

Sly paced back and forth, tugging on his dreads as if they would give some intuitive answers, some clarity from up high. "This is some cosmic bullshit…"

"You might want to start writing up a will, my nigga," Orlando said, leaning against the car.

"Naw not today, nigga. I know exactly what happened. We got jacked by a couple mogs. I knew I should've shot that nigga in the face when I had the chance. That's what happens when you don't finish a job. It comes back to bite you in the ass."

Orlando stared at Sly in disbelief. "How can you prove that?"

"It's a feeling…I mean it can't be coincidence they were right here before we came outside and the way they skirted off."

"Alright, let's say you're right and these little niggas did jack us, what are we going to do? O's going to kill me if he finds out I lost his money."

Sly ran his hands through his thick dreads. "First we're going to kill those niggas, and then we're going to get that money back and then we're dipping out of town."

Sly leaned against a fence, smoking a cigarette. He had been waiting for ten minutes. Taking out a fresh one, he took a deep inhale on his current smoke, feeling the nicotine rush through his body. It made him more alert, more focused.

Looks like I won't need this yet, he thought, placing the new cigarette back in his pocket.

A man rode his bike in the distance. Sly had watched this man for the last couple of days, tracing his movements and noting any variables in his routine. He knew this man's trajectory like the back of his hand.

The nigga in question went by the name of Key, and he DJed at house parties and a few clubs every weekend. He was starting to make a name for himself and knew just about everybody in the city.

Key rode by on his bike, air pods lodged in his ears, oblivious to Sly's presence.

Sly kicked the back tire and watched Key lose control of the bike, failing to brake in time. The airpods went flying, skidding into the street while Key fell on his left side and the bike slid into a fence.

"What the fuck, man?" Key said, rubbing his elbow.

Sly walked over with his phone in his hand and pistol in the other. He shoved the screen in Key's confused face.

"Just watch the video and shut up." Sly pressed play.

It showed Marcus sleeping on the train. Drool running out the corner of his mouth and his head tilted to the side. There was the sound of laughter in the background.

Under normal circumstances it would've been hilarious, but Sly's face was dead serious. Key looked at the video start to replay and he looked back down at the gun.

"Listen up, nigga. You know damn near everybody in Chicago. So don't lie to me when I ask you a simple question. You got it?"

"Yeah," Key said.

"Who is this?"

"I don't know, man."

Sly pistol-whipped Key across the face, breaking his nose. *Crunch.* Blood trickled out.

"That shit looks like it hurt. Probably not a good look for your image huh?"

Key looked around for some help, but the sidewalk was deserted and the people across the street seemed unbothered. Cars zoomed by, paying them no mind.

"Now I'm going to ask you again and you better tell me the truth. Who the fuck is this?" He raised the phone up to Key's busted face.

"Marcus."

"Okay, we're getting somewhere. And where can I find this *Marcus?*"

"I see him at the junkyard sometimes."

"There are lots of junkyards. I need the addy. Be specific."

"It's on Kostner Avenue. Across the street from Lucky Dog."

"Okay, I know where that's at. I might grab a hotdog and cheese fries after I pay your friend a visit."

Sly shoved Key on the sidewalk and aimed the gun at his chest.

"Don't think about telling that nigga either or it's your ass. You hear me?"

Key stared into Sly's hazel eyes and started backing up. Piss trickled down his leg. It looked as if he had seen the Devil himself.

12.
Freedom's Call

Zoe lounged on Gordo's couch. Kicking her feet in the air. Her thumbs moved across her phone's keypad at the speed of light as she played on her phone, scrolling through multiple apps.

She paused. "Do you ever worry about dying alone?"

"That's a heavy ass question," Marcus said.

"For real though. Do you?"

"Yeah, but I try not to think about it too much. Barely made it out of a shooting earlier this year. I'm tired."

"I'm glad you made it," she rubbed his neck, massaging the tension built up. "It's just something that nags me, you know. I've seen so many people drift apart and die. It's crazy. Almost as if the odds are stacked against us."

"You think too much."

"You got to," she said. "Have you seen this old lady online who dresses like she's still in her twenties?"

"Naw," Marcus said.

"She's got a ton of followers on social media. Her brand must be strong."

"Or maybe she just has a lot of money."

"Possibly, but that's beside the point."

"Does she still look good for her age?"

"Yeah, I mean her body still looks like a body." She held the phone up to Marcus' face.

Marcus gripped the phone and laughed.

Zoe moved closer to Marcus, feeling his warmth. "She looks about as good as you can for 90—I think. And she's got a charming aura about her. Good energy, you know?"

"I could see that. You think she's just trying to fit in or something? Relive her youth?"

"No, I think it's more than that. Not being constrained by societal norms and shit. It seems so freeing."

"Freedom. I'd like a toke of that."

Zoe punched Marcus in the shoulder. "Weed's good and all. But I'm talking about real freedom. You can see it in her eyes. The way she lets her shoulder fall. The lack of tension in her face."

Marcus scrolled through a few more photos, pausing on one. It was close-up of the lady's face. Her frosty blue eyes grew large, engulfing him. A chill ran down his spine and he wondered if this was what freedom felt like.

The scrapyard looked like something plucked straight out of a *Mad Max* ripoff. Old cars beyond repair dotted the fenced-in property like rusted sentinels. Engine blocks, fuel pumps, exhaust systems, dingy hubcaps, and hoses were strewn across the unkempt yard.

In the center of the automotive chaos, a small square concrete building stuck out like a blemish. Roger Atkins owned the scrapyard, and he'd been there as long as Gordo and Marcus could remember. He looked over this place as if it was his own child.

They used to bring copper and steel parts they'd strip from abandoned properties for extra cash. Once they got older, they targeted cars. The more valuable the part, the heftier the payday.

Once Marcus and Gordo stripped their first car together, Marcus knew they were finally Jackboys, baptized in oil and lean. Gordo had always been the more mechanically savvy of the two, but he taught Marcus everything he knew until he saw his movements mirrored his own and car tools became secondary appendages.

Marcus eased the car into the lot, crushing the tall grass and weeds spilling out the cracks. He shifted the keys to the right and the engine shut off.

A black muscular pitbull chained to wooden post ran back and forth, barking at Marcus and Gordo.

"I wish that dog would shut the fuck up," Gordo said.

"I thought you were a dog whisperer," Marcus said, shouldering the bag of parts.

"Roger's dog is bi-polar. One day it loves me, the next it wants to rip my head off. No whispering will do me any good."

"Sounds like every relationship you've been in."

"You make a good point. Fuck those bitches."

Roger came outside and put his hands on his hips. He was

an older man with laugh lines and watery brown eyes hidden behind a pair of cheap glasses. He wore a large t-shirt, but his muscles were still defined despite having a slight beer belly. The old man used to be a bodybuilder back in the day.

He sauntered over and embraced Marcus and Gordo.

"I see you boys brought gifts. Come in," he waved them inside. "Come in."

Marcus and Gordo followed him inside the cramped space. Gordo sat down on the couch, spreading himself out so he could take over the entire space.

Marcus sat down on a rollie chair and spun in a circle.

"Glad you two like to put your damn feet all over my furniture." Roger said, pointing mostly at Gordo.

"These kicks are clean though," Gordo said, moving his feet off the couch.

"I don't care how clean you think your shoes are. They don't belong on my furniture. Just when I think y'all are doing alright, you go crazy."

"My bad," Gordo said, taking his feet off the couch.

Marcus stalled his spinning and locked eyes with Roger.

"Okay, now that we got that out the way, we can get down to business. Let me see the goods," Roger said, rubbing his palms together.

Marcus unzipped the large bag and pulled out the hubcaps, sensors, airbag, and sound system.

Roger adjusted his glasses before picking up the hubcaps. He inspected them from front to back.

"I have no idea why you young niggas love some shiny

hubcaps so much. People should really invest their money in a better engine or a new interior. It's like throwing all your money at a colorful jacket rather than hitting the gym and getting yourself in shape."

Gordo shrugged and Marcus stayed silent.

Zoe's presence motivated Marcus. He found himself at work dreaming of her by his side and here he was dreaming of her intoxicating scent and gentle touch. He pictured them together, celebrating holidays with each other, traveling, etc. He'd get there soon enough.

Roger finished inspecting the gear and started putting it away.

"Y'all did good work. I'll give you a couple stacks for all this."

"Cool," Marcus said, dapping Gordo.

Roger unlocked a drawer underneath his desk and pulled out a stack of cash, licking his thumb as he counted out the bills. It was a weird tradition, but part of the ritual.

Gordo took the cash and counted it again. He nodded before splitting it halfway with Marcus. Everything straight down the middle.

13.
An Auctioneer's Torment

Roger logged onto an online auction website and checked on the car parts he had for sale. Looked like a few suckers bought them.

The parts brought in a steady stream of cash, and with young cats like Marcus and Gordo bringing him a fresh supply of parts on a frequent basis, he made a decent living. He had his dog, a decent collection of action figures, and a nice ride. That's all he really needed.

There was a heavy knock at the door. Roger leapt up from his chair and knocked his knee into his desk. A half cup of coffee spilled off the table and splattered on some paperwork.

"Goddamnit," he said, massaging his knee.

The front door opened, hinges groaning, and a young man with a head full of dreads and a cigarette dangling out of his mouth stood in the entrance staring at Roger. He was draped in black and grey clothing. The sun made his usually sharp features soft, hazy and doughy.

"No smoking in here, young man. Didn't you read the sign?"

"Fuck your sign, nigga."

"What do you want?" Roger asked, slowly opening his desk drawer.

"I need some information."

"Well I'm sure you heard of the internet. That has plenty of information and then some. We're not the only junkyard in town, you hear?"

The dreadhead laughed, moving up to the counter with an off-kilter walk. There was coiled tension brewing in every step forward.

Roger noticed the heart with wings tatted on the young man's neck and wondered what the significance was. He knew this young man had no love in his heart. Hate and chaos was emanating off him in waves.

"You got jokes, oldhead. I like that."

Roger shuffled through the papers in the drawers. Danger alarms ringing in his head.

Where the hell is my gun? he thought, growing nervous.

"I just want to ask a couple questions. Relax. I'm not here to hurt you."

"I don't know if I believe that."

"Well, if you just answer my questions I won't have to get violent, my nigga."

"Alright. What you want to know?"

"Have you seen a nigga named Marcus around here? A close associate of his told me he does *business* around here. Maybe I got the wrong junkyard."

Roger was surprised at how hot it was getting inside the

office. He tugged at the inside of his collar. A few flies buzzed overhead, and he smacked one, missing completely.

"I get a lot of customers coming through here. Hard for me to remember their names. Comes with age."

"Listen oldhead, I know you don't know me, but I get really angry when someone lies to me. I know they're just words, but they mean a lot to me. All I ask for is the truth. A little honesty and integrity goes a long way. Now where the hell is Marcus?"

"I don't know."

"Okay, I'm done playin with you, oldhead."

Roger hadn't gotten into a scuffle in about a good year and a half, and the last time he wrestled was twenty years ago. Still, he outweighed the intruder by at least thirty pounds.

He moved in front of the counter and charged the dreadhead, tackling him against the wall. Better to be on the offensive. Something popped in his shoulder.

Not good. Not good at all.

Roger applied pressure, pinning the young man against the wall. He let off and threw a wild elbow and missed.

The young man caught Roger in the jaw with a right hook. It was sloppily thrown, but still did some damage. Roger staggered backward, nursing his jaw. Hoped he wouldn't have to get looked at after this.

The young man took advantage of the opening and pulled out his gun, waving it in the air.

"Enough of this hand-to-hand shit. If you don't tell me what I want to know I'm just going shoot your brains out on this floor. And then I'm going out front and I'm going to shoot your dog. That's on gang, nigga."

Roger wished he had his gun right now. He'd blow this nigga to kingdom come. The young folk were so entitled these days and lacked respect for their elders. When Hoover was out of jail, there were rules, structure, a code. This had disintegrated into a goddamn circus over the decades.

"It's okay. You don't have to talk. My girl Nina would love to sing you a lullaby," He looked at his .9mm with a wry softness. "Wouldn't you, baby?"

"Alright. Alright. I might know a Marcus."

"You might know?"

The dreadhead aimed the gun at Roger and pulled the trigger.

Boom.

The gun shot was deafening, and Roger crumpled to the ground, a flash of heat lodged in his lower body. He stared in sheer disbelief at the fresh hole in his knee. Blood gushed out. Nothing could have prepared him for the excruciating pain spiraling out of his knee, and the agonizing yell exiting his mouth.

"Get wishy washy with me again nigga and I'll blow out your other knee. You got me?"

Roger spoke through gritted teeth. "Yeah."

"I'm glad we're on the same page. Now where is Marcus?"

Roger bit his lip until it bled. He didn't want to say the names, but he was scared. The fear spread through his core like a rampant virus, growing stronger by the minute. It was moving upward, reaching for his throat.

Roger swallowed the fear down, forcing it into small box in his mind.

"Marcus hangs out with this bigger fella named Gordo. He works at a car shop. You'll probably find him there."

"Hmmm...I don't like the word *probably,* but I believe you. I can smell a lie, nigga. Remember that and let those niggas know I'm coming for what's mine."

The dreadhead walked out the door and let it slam behind him.

Roger applied a copious amount of hydrogen peroxide to his cuts. He drank enough whiskey to kill a hobo. He had already packed his shit in two pieces of luggage and got his papers in order.

His hands shook as scrolled through the contacts on his phone. He had to tell the youngins death was coming for them. He wasn't sure if he could bear being the messenger of bad news, but it was the least could do.

It had to be done. He felt guilty that he cracked and let their names slip off his tongue. He was the worst type of scum and a coward at that.

He dialed Marcus' number and each ring sounded like a death bell in his mind.

Ringing. Ringing. Ringing. Ringing. Ringing. Ringing.

"Aye Roger, what's good?" Marcus said.

"Got some bad news."

"Lay it on me."

"Someone wants you and Gordo dead."

"Hol up. Who wants me dead?"

"A dreadhead with a star on his face and a heart on his neck. He blew my knee out. Came here causing a ruckus about you. I'm surprised I can still hobble around my place."

"Oh shit, do you want me to come through and slide?" Marcus asked, ready.

"No, I don't want you coming anywhere near me. Could be dangerous. Nigga could be watching right now. Probably holed up in one of the gutted cars smoking. But you need get out of town or hide somewhere. This nigga wants you dead and I let your names slip."

"You let our names slip?" Marcus voice went up a few notches. "I thought you were an OG. How could you do this?"

"I'm sorry. I truly am. But he had a gun and he fucked me up. *Bad.* My knee is blown out...and I don't have health insurance..."

"Fuckfuckfuckfuck," Marcus said, trying to catch his breath on the other end.

"You know these niggas are savages. No code. No order. Just wyling out in the streets."

"You're right."

"I got some family in Atlanta. I'm going to grab my shit and head down there. I don't need this man coming back to finish me off. You can come with me if you want."

"Naw, my mom's up here, and I got a girl. I have to handle this situation head-on. What else you tell him?"

"I told him he might find you at the car shop."

"Fuck," Marcus said, hitting something in the background.

"I'm sorry, Marcus."

"Sorry ain't gonna cut it, nigga. I feel bad that he fucked you up, but you told him everything. We might as print out some shirts with my face on it."

"There's always a solution. Remember that and stay safe."

Marcus hung up.

Roger threw the phone across the room. He slumped to the floor, cradling his knee to his chest. The pain was too much to bear. He thought about just ending himself then and there, but he couldn't go through with it.

He took another swig and sobbed until the windows darkened. He stood and left the junkyard, waving goodbye to his second home.

14.
A Prelude to Judgment Day

Marcus and Zoe sat on a bench staring up at the waxing crescent moon. Zoe nuzzled her head into the crook of his neck and felt his pulse through her ear.

It was still warm out, and she listened to him complain about work. This had become a daily routine. He smelled like dryer sheets and cologne. She pulled a plastic baggie out of her purse and waved it in front of him.

Marcus' eyes widened.

"What's that?"

"Some loud."

"My nigga."

Zoe took out some rolling papers and laid them over her skirt. She took the weed out the bag and sprinkled just the right amount on top of the papers. Licking the edges, she sealed the blunt.

"You should do the honors." She handed Marcus the lighter and the blunt.

Marcus pulled softly and inhaled the smoke. Coughing, he bent over, banging his chest.

"Damn…(cough)…you didn't lie. This shit hits."

"I told you." She grabbed the blunt and took a puff. She exhaled the smoke through her nostrils.

Zoe watched Marcus melt into the bench. Time seemed to slow down. Her senses sharpened and honed into the sounds of cars racing by and the birds fluttering in an oak tree behind them.

She held Marcus' hand, feeling the lines in his palm, wondering if she showed up in the soft ridges, and swore she could feel his blood running underneath his skin like a subtle current.

After taking another toke, Marcus grabbed his chest with his free hand.

"What's wrong babe?" she said.

"Feels like I grew a second heart."

She didn't mean to, but she laughed. It was contagious. Marcus doubled over laughing, but still held his imaginary heart in his chest.

"If you're not careful, I just might snatch that heart out your chest. Show you some real magic," she said.

Marcus gained his composure and wiped tears from his eyes. "Hitting stains on my heart. You're a good one."

"What do you think of the loud though? You like it?" she said, pulling on the blunt, nearly finished.

"It's good. Feels like cobwebs are in my stomach and my arms are heavy. Where'd you get it?"

"The plug, nigga."

They both laughed and melted into one another, lightly kissing.

"Can you tell me something?"

"Sure."

"Can you tell me a secret? Something no one else knows."

Marcus spent a couple minutes, sifting through his past. "I got one, but promise you won't tell anyone. And I mean anyone."

Zoe nodded responding in a soft tone. "I promise."

"And promise you won't judge me.

"I promise."

"Me and Gordo came up on a bag of money."

"How?"

"We stole it."

Zoe sat up, wanting to hear more. "Hold on, you stole it from where?"

Marcus took a deep breath. "We got lucky and stumbled on it while we were out on a job. Whoever it was left it in the backseat. Car doors unlocked and everything. Can you believe that shit?"

"No, that's crazy. I mean I had no idea you were hitting stains like that. I knew there was something off about you."

"Damn, why I gotta be off?"

"Don't take it personally. We're all a little off and I think it's sexy to be honest."

"You do?"

"Yeah."

They kissed once again before Zoe continued the conversation. "How much money are we talking?"

"Let's just say I can pay for your college tuition, my college tuition, and Gordo's college tuition if I felt like it."

"Get out."

"I swear."

Zoe pictured stacks on stacks on stacks, almost growing dizzy at the thought of counting that money by hand. "There's so much you could do with that amount of money."

"I know."

Zoe snuggled up with Marcus, leaned her head on his chest, allowing him to cradle her. She closed her eyes, dreaming of money.

I can't call it.

Marcus didn't know what to do, but he knew how to pick the lock to his mom's crib. He'd recently got into an argument with her about weed she found in his room, so he was staying with Gordo. He didn't know why he hadn't moved out a long time ago.

He fished a credit card from his wallet, one that he yanked off some out-of-towner the other night, and shoved it in the door jamb. He slid it downward until he felt the locking mechanism begin to give and jimmied it until the latch slid open.

"Yessir." He pushed the door open.

He listened for any signs of his Mom, but she wasn't there. Living with her for the last 19 years, he knew her movements and routine by heart. It was Sunday morning, so of course she would be at church, praising the Lord.

He went to the closet and tossed a pile of clothes to the side and found the shoebox that used to house his red Supras. He sold those awhile back.

He went back to his door and made sure it was locked. Didn't need his mom strolling in here and freaking out. He gently took the lid off the box and placed it to the side.

Inside lay his black Beretta M9. His uncle gave it to him on his 17th birthday, knowing Marcus got into nefarious activities. His uncle stressed the importance of carrying the piece and when to use it. It was meant to be a last resort, and it looked like Marcus had no other option but to put it to use.

Marcus held the Beretta in his hands, getting used to that familiar weight again. He never actually had to use it for real, but he practiced shooting in abandoned homes to keep sharp.

He was still wary about the thought of using it. He wasn't sure if he was prepared to take a man's life. Shoving the piece in his waistband, he realized he should give his uncle a call. The old man had a wealth of advice, especially when it came to potential trouble.

Marcus snuck out the front door and jogged down the stairs. They groaned with age. He pulled out his cellphone and dialed his uncle Jimmy.

His uncle picked up on the fifth ring and answered in a gruff voice, "Talk to me."

"It's Marcus."

"Ice, how you doin? We haven't talked in a hunnid years."

"I'm not doing so hot to be honest. Got into a bit of… trouble."

"What happened? A girl break your heart? You behind on a bill? You got fired from that hotel job?"

"Naw, nothing like that. My girl situation is fine."

"You got yourself a girlfriend?"

"Yeah. You'd like her. She's cute and smart."

"Might have to bring her over one day so I can check her out."

"Bet."

"Tell me about this issue you got. I can hear the stress all up in your voice. Must be pretty serious."

Marcus sighed. He wasn't sure how to phrase the situation properly, or if he should just let it all out. "Let's just say I'm in some deep shit. I jacked something big and the owner wants my head."

"Fuck," Jimmy said. "Anyone important?"

"Some dreadhead nigga. He's a GD. Have no idea who he is though, but he's causing issues looking for me. Like it's a manhunt or something crazy."

"That is a problem. Gimme a sec to think this through."

"Alright."

After some shuffling on the other line, Jimmy started speaking again. "You can leave town. Maybe catch a bus to Indiana. You got some cousins out there who might take you in. Might be your only option."

"I don't wanna leave though. Me and Mom aren't on the best of terms right now. But I have my girl here and my nigga Gordo always holds me down. I'd just feel like a coward if I dipped out. I want to stand my ground for once. There has to be another way."

"You still got that birthday gift I gave you, right?"

"Yeah. Got it on me right now. Paranoid as shit."

"That's good to hear. Not the paranoid part, but you know what I mean. Stay in public places and keep your head down. You might have to take a break from jacking motherfuckers every weekend. Maybe just stick to your job at the hotel and this will blow over."

"Yeah but this nigga knows my name. Reps GDs, remember?"

"You got some balls hitting licks on gang members. No wonder we're related." Jimmy laughed.

Marcus smiled weakly. He didn't have the juice to laugh right now. Too much shit was weighing him down.

"I didn't know I was jacking dude. I thought it was some random nigga. A stain."

"You gotta be more careful."

"I know."

"How bad does he want your head?" Jimmy said.

"Pretty bad."

"Well if you ain't leaving the city…looks like you might have to kill the nigga."

15.
Strapped Up

Marcus rubbed his bloodshot eyes. "I don't know man. We gotta do something."

"Okay. I'm cool with playing offense, but neither of us has caught a body. Think about it like this though: you got your girl and your mom to think about. I don't really have any family. I'm on my own. And to tell you the truth, you're the only nigga I truly fuck with. On gawd. Maybe you should take the majority of the money and dip out."

"I appreciate that fam, and I don't use the word *fam* lightly. I'm just stressed out. And you don't need to sacrifice yourself for nobody especially me. Erase that completely…I've thought this through about a thousand times and I keep picturing us dying. I don't want either of us ending up on the news as another statistic."

Gordo puffed on his black and mild and blew out a cloud of smoke. It made the whole world go hazy for moment.

Seeing his best friend's pensive face and furrowed brows brought him back down to reality. They had to do something.

It was just a matter of time before the dreadhead would come knocking on their door.

"We gotta strap up. There's no other option."

"What did you have in mind?" Marcus asked.

Gordo dipped into his bedroom to retrieve an AR-15 from under the mattress. Slapped a fresh clip in and took another puff of his black and mild.

"I got a loose plan," he said. "And this time, we won't be caught lacking."

16.
Alternative Trouble

Sly pulled up to the auto shop. He had planned to come earlier, but Chicago traffic slowed him down dramatically. Time was of the essence.

"You ready?" Sly asked.

Orlando pulled on his black ski mask and nodded. "You already know."

Sly looked through the holes in his mask and observed the auto shop. The parking lot had a couple cars in it, but seemed otherwise empty.

"What's the move?" Orlando asked.

"We wait."

"Let's run up on those niggas."

"They know we're coming through."

A car horn honked and Sly looked around, seeking out the person doing the honking.

Honk. Honk. Honkkkkkkkkk.

"Who the fuck?" Orlando said, growing furious.

A car revved its engine and Sly saw Marcus in his peripheral.

He was parallel parked on the adjacent street with a shitty grin plastered on his face and a middle finger in the air.

"That motherfucker, Marcus."

Marcus pulled off, slowly moving into traffic. Sly turned the car around with the quickness, tailing Marcus.

"Looks like Marcus is on his own," Orlando said. "Probably carrying heat."

"Is he dumb or is there more to this?"

Orlando cocked his gun, ready to let his choppa sing. "It doesn't matter."

Sly pushed down on the accelerator, and they both hit a red light. Marcus was a few cars ahead, looking forward. Slamming on the brakes, the car lurched forward and fell back, weight distribution settling out. He gripped the steering wheel and his perception swam in a woozy motion.

What the hell is this feeling?

Déjà fuckin vu.

Sly felt like he had lived this moment before. Maybe he dreamed this in the past or experienced this before. A hazy recollection gnawing at the edge of his conscious mind. The light turned green and he continued trailing Marcus, exiting onto the expressway.

It wasn't high speed chase, more of a calm drive, weaving between cars and keeping a good pace. Memories flooded Sly's mind while his body was on cruise control, going through the motions. He was brought back to his pre-teens with Orlando, long before they lost their innocence, long before they became GD, a time when they were just kids having fun.

"You're dead, nigga."

"Naw, you only got me in my arm. I can't die from that."

Sly aimed his watergun at Orlando's knobby knees, pulling the trigger. A stream of warm water hit his friend's lower body. Orlando screamed out, and fell over feigning a major wound.

"Got you nigga," Sly laughed.

"Look what you did. Now I'm a parapalogic."

"You mean paraplegic?"

"Yeah, that."

They continued shooting the guns at each other, shirts soaked, ducking behind trees and bushes for cover.

Another kid named Victor from across the street came pedaling down the sidewalk, watching them have fun.

"Hey dumb fucks. What are you doing?"

"What's it look like, nigga?" Orlando said.

"And who are you calling dumb?" Sly said.

"Did I stutter?" Victor placed his hands on his hips.

Sly shot the watergun at Victor, hitting him in the face. Anger boiled in Victor's balled up fists. He was embarrassed as if they had shot God himself in the face.

"You two fucked up."

Orlando and Sly laughed.

"This isn't funny." Victor ran forward and shoved Orlando.

Sly jumped on his Victor's back, weighing the kid down who was one year older than him and his friend. He punched his ribcage over and over.

Orlando got up, brushing grass off, and kicked Victor in the face.

"Fuck nigga should have left us alone."

Sly spit on Victor as he got up to assess the damage of his handiwork.

Victor's face was a mess, a patchwork of bruises already forming an abstract painting. Blood dribbled out of his crooked nose.

"Damn nigga," Orlando said, struggling to contain his laughter. "You got fucked up."

Victor cried and slowly got back up to his feet, the masculine vigor gone.

"I-I'm going to tell my brother and he's going to kill both of you. You'll regret this. I promise."

Orlando and Sly laughed while dapping each other up.

"We'll be waiting," Sly said.

Victor's brother was a Latin King who made good on his promise and fucked them up one day after school in an alley. Bruised and battered, they walked home together. Nothing could tear them apart. No fist, no threat, no gun. They were inseparable.

Sly followed Marcus off an exit. They were passing cornfield after cornfield and had spent at least half a tank on this chase.

"Where is this nigga taking us?" Orlando said, right knee bouncing up and down.

"I don't know." Sly said.

Marcus put on his turn signal, turning left into a junkyard. Sly followed suit and slowly pulled into the junkyard. A large sign with crows perched on the edge loomed overhead— *Scrappys*.

"This gives me a bad feeling," Orlando said, squeezing his gun.

"I know."

"What city are we in?"

"Plainfield. Saw a sign a while back. Niggas brought us to the middle of nowhere."

Marcus disappeared into the lines of rusted cars, some of them gutted while others looked like relics of the yesteryear. Automotive stillborns, blending into the cornfield. A mechanical graveyard.

The junkyard was silent, overgrown weeds swaying in the wind. Fat bees hovering over the flowers dotting the desolate landscape.

Pop. Pop. Pop.

Sly and Orlando ducked down, covering their heads instinctually. They waited a couple minutes before coming up for air. Sly tried moving the car forward, but they were at a standstill.

"Fucking flat tire," Orlando said.

"Keep your eyes focused. That fat nigga Gordo's posted."

"Don't worry about that n—"

Pop. Pop.

The windshield cracked in multiple places. Two gaping holes allowed a warm wind to swell inside the car.

"Nigga, don't you dare die on me," Sly wrapped his arm around Orlando, leaning his head on his shoulder. Two gunshot wounds were bleeding out of his friend's heaving chest. It all happened so fast.

Sly wiped a tear from his eye with his tatted knuckle, free

hand still gripping his gun. *Shaking.* They'd been friends since middle school. Went through initiation the same day. Nothing could tear them apart.

"I'm not gonna make it, Sly."

"I know."

"Kill these niggas. For me. For GD."

"You know I got you."

"Promise me something."

"Name it."

"Get out the city."

"I will. I promise. I'll find a way out. After I kill these niggas."

"GD till the world blow."

Orlando went pale in the face, and he stopped breathing. Sly held his friend's warm head in his arms and it felt like a heavy weight. Checked for a pulse just to make sure he wasn't hallucinating.

Sly hugged his friend close and kissed him on the forehead, disturbed by the lack of a heartbeat.

"Fuck niggas," he muttered.

Sly got out the car and ducked down, waiting for more shots. After a few moments, nothing happened. He thought about creeping out into the open, but knew better.

Another rally of shots rocked the car and fluids leaked out, forming a puddle on the asphalt. The smell of gasoline was thick in the air.

Sly stood up like a cobra ready to strike anyone who got in his way. Adrenaline raced through his veins, and he couldn't remember the last time he took his pills. Anger coursed through his body. He felt like he didn't need any medication. He needed retribution. He needed vengeance.

He couldn't control his emotions, the rage spilling out his pores.

"Come out of hiding you fuck niggas."

Sly shot his gun in the sky, unloading the full clip, hoping to bring everything down with it.

Pop. Pop. Pop.

"You missed me, you dumb niggas."

Sly knew death was on his heels despite his statement. He readied himself, hoping his friend was waiting for him on the otherside. One shot ignited the car's fluid behind him. A white blinding light and a searing heat consumed Sly's world entirely.

The remnants of a charred paper crane floated in the wind. Pointed head still intact.

Fade to white.

Gordo massaged his sore shoulder. "Kickback was crazy."

"Didn't know you were celebrating the 4th of July?"

Marcus and Gordo hugged each other. They moved like old weary soldiers, staggering towards Gordo's whip.

Gordo cruised in relative silence, glancing at Marcus, who looked like he was ready to pass out.

"What are you going to do about the bodies?" Marcus asked.

"Don't worry about it. I know people."

"You gonna be alright?"

"Yeah, I'll be fine. I'm more worried about you. Get some sleep. Chill with Zoe. Try to relax. We'll figure things out in the morning."

Gordo dropped Marcus off and he went inside, ready to pass out. He chugged a bottle of water and found the duffle bag on the living room table. He sat down on the couch and unzipped it.

Half the money was gone.

He dug through the stacks of cash and found a book of poems by Apollo Jones buried at the bottom. *Black Gypsies.*

He opened the front cover and a notecard slipped out. An address scribbled in purple gel ink. The potent smell of loud weed rose from the pages.

Marcus looked back at the open page and read the poem.

"Area 773"

Jellyfish fly over the projects like ufos,
This isn't Roswell, but here they are nonetheless,
Blame it on the purple kush,
tendrils of smoke
curling round

"Hell naw," my sister says pointing at the translucent bodies,
Tentacles gliding over rooftops,
We reach out hoping they will abduct us,
Take us away to a foreign space

No dice, they float on
"Fuck em, fuck em, fuck em,"
My favorite mantra,
I wonder if the jellyfish can see my middle finger,
waving like a brown flag in the night

Marcus grinned. "Ain't that some shit."

ACKNOWLEDGMENTS

Special thanks to JDO for believing in me, being patient with my ass, and giving my book a home, Kelby Losack for the constant encouragement and putting the literary battery in my back, Michael Kazepis for pushing me to be authentic, David Simmons for the support, Nami, Chicago, Lil Durk, Yeezus, Lucki, William Pauley III, Scott Adlerberg, Daniel Vlasaty, Sharonda, Twilight, Jean Deaux, Jordan Harper, Teep, Michael J. Seidlinger, Daniel Meshel, Jeremy Robert Johnson, Fredo, Benoit Lelievre, Joseph Bouthiette Jr., Takashi Miike, Coyote Black, Saba, the Safdie Brothers, good weed, and the universe.

Twitter: @grantmirage
IG: @_grantmirage

Grant Wamack is the author of *God's Leftovers, A Lightbulb's Lament,* and *Notes from the Guts of a Hippo.* He has had more than 40 short stories published in places such as *Dark Moon Digest, the Best of Surreal Grotesque,* and *The New Flesh.* When he's not writing, he's reading tarot cards, rapping, practicing jiu jitsu, and smoking weed in LA. You can visit his website here: http://www.grantwamack.wordpress.com

Visit brokenriverbooks.com for our full catalogue.

Thank you for picking up this title.

Fucking good, right?